Under The North Star

The Underground Railroad in Olde Sandwich Towne

Joanna Bullard

Copyright © 2014 by Joanna Bullard
First Edition — August 2014

ISBN
978-1-4602-4323-7 (Hardcover)
978-1-4602-4324-4 (Paperback)
978-1-4602-4325-1 (eBook)

All rights reserved.

No part of this publication may be reproduced in any form, or by any means, electronic or mechanical, including photocopying, recording, or any information browsing, storage, or retrieval system, without permission in writing from the publisher.

Produced by:

FriesenPress
Suite 300 — 852 Fort Street
Victoria, BC, Canada V8W 1H8

www.friesenpress.com

Distributed to the trade by The Ingram Book Company

FOREWORD	xiii
PROLOGUE: September, 1838:	xv
June, 1840: CHAPTER 1	1
October, 1843: CHAPTER 2	13
November 1843 CHAPTER 3	35
April 1844 CHAPTER 4	55
April, 1845 CHAPTER 5	81
August, 1846 CHAPTER 6	93
March 1849 CHAPTER 7	137
September 1851 EPILOGUE	153
Post Script	157

**This book is dedicated to my sons,
Doug and Chris.**

FriesenPress has been instrumental in this publication. I am grateful for all their advice concerning the editing, design, promotion and publishing of this manuscript.

Under The North Star

An Olde Sandwich Towne Story

PSALM 121

1. I will lift up mine eyes unto the hills, from whence cometh my help.

2. My help cometh from the Lord, which made heaven and earth.

3. He will not suffer thy foot to be moved: He
   that keepeth thee will not slumber.

4. Behold, He that keepeth Israel shall neither slumber nor sleep.

5. The Lord is thy keeper: the Lord is thy shade upon thy right hand.

6. The sun shall not smite thee by day, nor the moon by night.

7. The Lord shall preserve thee from all evil: He shall preserve thy soul.

8. The Lord shall preserve thy going out and thy coming
   in from this time forth, and even for evermore.

FOREWORD

THE FOLLOWING STORY IS A WORK OF FICTION. I HAVE USED the names of some of my friends and family, but the characters they portray, and the situations where they find themselves, bear no relation to any person I know. The story runs from 1838 to 1851 and will portray situations that happened during that time in Olde Sandwich Towne, which is located in West Windsor, Ontario, Canada.

I have done some research, and tried to make the story accurate as far as the situation of those times. I have mentioned some historical facts and people of the times, however many situations are just not known, and I have concocted a story of my own imagination. Some of the details of the facts may or may not have actually occurred at that time.

I know it is true, however, that residents of Sandwich Village, Amherstburg, and the Essex County area, with the cooperation of the Chippewa People hid escaped refugees from the Southern United States from 'slave catchers', sent by their previous 'owners'. They also helped them with food, new clothing, and to move further inland for more safety when the situation warranted. I know the residents in this area, helped the refugees who felt safe here plant roots, and helped them deal with life in a new land.

Furthermore, not everyone in this area welcomed the newcomers. Some white people here had beliefs similar to the Southern landowners. All places to live have their challenges. Sometimes, the fleeing person has problems follow them, as in the several cases where 'slave catchers' crossed the border to catch or replace slaves they were chasing.

In 1834 Upper Canada formally enacted the Emancipation Proclamation which officially ended slavery in Canada. By this time many people no longer agreed with the practice; and most of those former slaves who were in Canada had begun living and working as independent and free people several years before.

Compared to the United States, Canada never had as many slaves. In Sandwich Town, on the Detroit River, West of Windsor, and North of Amherstburg, in Essex County a settlement was growing. They had white neighbours, and native neighbours. Everyone worked to make their way toward a better and more comfortable life.

By 1838, small businesses were sprouting up in the town, along 'main street', Sandwich Road, which started to follow the Detroit River and then headed further inland, but still following the river.

Long narrow farms fronted on the river also in the French style; after all, the French had originally settled the area in the 1600's. A Band of native people, the Chippewa lived downstream from Sandwich. It was mostly a farming community at that time. Since slavery was still legal in the United States; the influx of refugees from the South had been crossing the river to escape for some time now. The main landing points of the Underground Railroad in Ontario, or at that time, Upper Canada, were in the Niagara Falls area, Amherstburg, and Sandwich/Windsor.

Life is just that, life. There are good people and bad people everywhere. When a person flees one situation for a better life from a place of physical slavery, how can they really know where they are going? Freedom is making choices. When a person has never been allowed to make life choices; sometimes even that freedom can be overwhelming.

A severe change of climate can also be a living breathing force to be reckoned with, if a person is not prepared to tackle the change. Many people are still shocked even today with plenty of information at their disposal, when they experience their first winter.

In this story, the main character considers a divorce. During this time Upper Canada, changed its name to Canada West and had also decided the marriage vows should be considered permanent. Divorce cases had to be read three times in the House of Commons, and be investigated by a Parliamentary Committee. Between 1840 and 1867 only four cases were ever waged, and only three divorces granted. It was a time consuming and expensive endeavour with little chance of success.

I also touch on the paternalistic society of that time, found in many countries, (and even now in some places) and the legal and emotional stresses placed upon women. Just how broad should we cast the definition of oppression?

The gripping question is, however: is there really a safe haven anywhere? My own belief is that the only real safe haven is in the loving arms of God, our Father in heaven.

Enjoy, and God bless.
Joanna Bullard

PROLOGUE:
September, 1838:

BANG!

Thump, thump, thump — down the back porch, to the barn.
Clip clop, clip clop — of hurried hooves down the lane.
Silence — it's over.

Ruth Logan sank down the side of the cupboards to the kitchen floor; her hands cradling her stomach and the almost eight month baby growing inside. Her seven year old son, Daniel slept through the argument in the next room; at least, she hoped he did.

Tense muscles unwilling to move, rolled her over, and she fell into a fitful sleep on the floor.

※

About a quarter mile down the road Sarah and Peter Berry watched Martin Logan cantor down the road away from home. "Again", they thought, "what's he up to this time?"

"We'll have to check on Ruth and Daniel in the morning." Sarah said.

"You'll have to do that alone. I must go down to the Band and find out if they have someone travelling inland. The new arrivals hiding at Pastor Hubbs' farm won't be safe this close to the river for long; their old owners have sent some 'catchers' after them. I'll ask Siwili (Tail of The Fox) if their sentries noticed Martin passing. I should also go to Amherstburg, and tell Ruth's Uncle Samuel he left again." Peter said.

Peter Berry, a black settler, became friends with Samuel Patterson while he was working on the farm next to Samuel's in Amherstburg. After sharing his dream of owning his own farm and being more involved in the project of helping refugees from the South, Peter and Samuel made a deal. Peter would purchase the two plots of Samuel's land next to Ruth and Martin Logan's farm. Ruth's Uncle Samuel carried the mortgage for them.

The Berry family: Peter, and Sarah, their son, Josh, who was Daniel's age, and a new addition to their family a daughter, Anna, who was born to them last year. The family was settling into an independent life.

Further down the road other eyes didn't miss Martin's departure either.

✦

Ruth Logan wasn't really ready for morning. Sleeping on the floor left her stiff and making her way to the 'back of the house' to relieve herself was a struggle. "More trips now the baby is growing." She thought.

Today, Ruth felt much older than her twenty-six years. She had a small build, brown eyes and dark brown wavy hair which now hung down her back in a long braid. Her Scottish heritage, blessed her with fair skin although working on the farm in the summer left it a little tanned. She liked to wear a large-brimmed hat to shade her face and eyes from the strong summer sun.

Her hat was indoors right now; the sun wasn't high in the sky yet. It was mid-September, the days were getting shorter, and the nights were starting to get cooler. She still wore her long flowing cotton nightgown from last night. It was going to be a warm and clear day; though she didn't really feel up to working outdoors today.

She would have to plan for this baby without Martin around and work had to be done in the house to rid their room of his things. She planned to keep the new baby with her in her room for now. That way, Daniel could have his room to himself for a while longer. How was Daniel going to cope without a father around?

Last night's argument played over, and over in her mind. She couldn't understand how much she had misjudged his character. Why did she think he had the same feelings about abolition as she did? He didn't even like to cooperate and trade with the Band people. He disagreed with Uncle Samuel's several dealings with the People from the Band and his long-time friendship with the local leader, Siwili.

"Heavens," She said out loud. "They were here first!"

She thought to herself again. Martin acted as if we were first, and they were the interlopers! Was she so taken with the idea of being in love with a handsome man from out of town she was blind to his real beliefs?

When she first saw him at the church social she was stricken. He was four years older than she, and his light brown hair and laughing Irish eyes charmed her. They walked in the garden nearby the church and talked. He seemed so self-assured, happy and contented with his life here in Essex County.

He was working on a neighbouring apple orchard at the time, and willingly accepted Uncle Samuel's offer to work one of his farm tracts near Sandwich Town after their marriage. She never even got to meet his family; he said they couldn't come down from Toronto for their wedding. After they were married, he never seemed to want to visit his family, and they never seemed to find time to visit here. Lately, she was wondering if it was even the truth.

Martin went to the local Methodist Church in Amherstburg with her and her Aunt and Uncle regularly when he was courting her, but, once they were married, she didn't understand the change in him. His whole outlook on life seemed to change. He wasn't interested in life at the local church in Sandwich, or on the farm, and did nothing but criticize the people down here.

He wanted Uncle Samuel to give him more responsibility in his business dealings, and lost all interest in the farm they were supposed to be running. At least Uncle Samuel still let them live on this tract of land he owned. At first she wondered why he didn't just give it to them as a wedding present. Now she understood Uncle Samuel must have wondered about Martin's real objectives.

After Daniel was born, Martin seemed proud, and she thought things would work out for a while. After abolition in the British Empire, and more refugees from slavery started coming up from the South, Martin's general bad mood seemed to worsen. It was as if he was threatened by their new-found freedom, and even their presence.

For the last several years, Martin had been leaving for several months at a time, and wouldn't talk about where he was going or what he'd been doing. He said if Uncle Samuel wasn't going to treat him like family, then he would make arrangements for our future by himself. Just what that meant, Ruth didn't know, and secretly she was worried. She knew she would not allow her or her children to leave Essex County, and her Aunt and Uncle. She just didn't know what her future held.

When Martin came back from that last mysterious trip the big trouble started. He found Peter and Sarah living on the two adjoining farm tracts next to them. Martin was furious.

"Why did your Uncle make arrangements to hold the mortgage for them, and we have to farm on land we don't own? We are blood, and they're not! Your Uncle should have given us all this land outright. It's not that he can't afford to give it to us!" Martin roared.

"That's it." She thought, as she purposefully closed the door to the outhouse after her, and brought her mind back to the present. She stood up straight, and steeled herself for the day ahead.

"Martin said he's gone for good this time so be it. I'll find my way with my children somehow."

She washed her hands and splashed some water on her face at the well. She gathered some eggs from the hen house and a bucket of milk from their cow. Then she headed for the house.

In the house, she left the food in the kitchen, and went into her bedroom to put on one of the 'roomy' dresses she saved from her first pregnancy. She then headed back into the kitchen to start breakfast for her and Daniel.

"It's daytime already." Daniel thought, "Momma and Poppa argued again last night. This time Poppa said he's not coming back. Why does he mind Momma helping the refugees? Why shouldn't she help by letting them work around the farm for food and shelter; and hire them for harvest time? He's angry; 'You've always let them hang around since we've been married!' Poppa roared from the kitchen where they argued.

"I remember ever since I was little always having someone to talk to. There has always been someone to help around the farm. Poppa says: 'Why do you have to take in the ones from the South?' I don't know why he's so angry — we're all God's children aren't we? That's what Pastor Burke said."

Daniel had light brown hair like his father, though it might darken as he grew older. This morning, he sat up and stretched with his arms reaching as high as he could. Then he ran his fingers through the loose silky curls on his head which tossed wildly with the movement of his fingers.

He was in a growth spurt right now, skinny, and taller, Ruth had to replace his pants and shirts this summer again before school started. She was expecting him to fill out again for a while then grow again, as he seemed to do. Usually, his eyes laughed easily like his father's used to. This morning Daniel was thoughtful.

Daniel thought about how his friend Josh and his folks lived in the old bunkhouse at the side of the barn until they got their house built on their new farm, the next down the road. It was an exciting time for everybody, the whole community helped when the Berry's new house and barn was being built. The men even let Daniel and Josh help out wherever they could, and the two boys felt so important and grown up. Now the Berry's have their own farm next to the Logan's.

"Josh is my very best friend." He thought. "Now that the new school year has started we go to school together every day. Good thing his folks got their house built before Poppa came back from that last trip! He would've been real angry to find a whole family in our bunkhouse. Course Josh spent lots of nights with me in my room! It was almost like having a brother — I wonder if Momma's new baby will be a boy or a girl."

He lay on his back in his bed, with his arms cupped under his head on the pillow. He wondered about how his life would change with the new baby, and now that his father was gone for good.

"Momma's moving around in the kitchen, guess I'd better get ready for breakfast and school." Slowly, he sat up in the bed, as his feet dangled over the side of his bed he tried to mentally prepare to face the unknown days ahead.

Soon, Ruth and Daniel sat at the table eating their breakfast of eggs and homemade raisin bread, with tea for her and milk for Daniel.

Ruth said: "Poppa left again last night. I think he's not coming back this time."

"I heard him Momma; we'll be okay, I'm getting bigger now and I can do more work around the farm."

"You're such a big help already, and you're only seven, but I want you to be a child as long as you can." Ruth felt guilty about Daniel hearing her and Martin quarrel, maybe now he won't have to hear them at it again.

They stopped talking when the clip-clop of horses' hooves, the jiggle of a wagon and joy-filled strains of singing came from outside their front door.

"O, a little talk wid Jesus, makes it right, all right." Sarah Berry, Josh, and the toddler, Anna drove up in their buckboard.

Sarah loved to sing, and was always teaching them the songs she was learning from the new Baptist church down the road some of the refugees started. They were meeting at the Pastor's farm house.

Daniel jumped up from his chair to run outside and greet them. Ruth rose, and left the table also, but she stayed on the front porch. She placed her hands on her hips, tilted her head to one side and smiled at the happy visitors. Daniel joined in the song as he ran out to join them.

"Troubles of every kind, Thank God, I'll always find, Dat a little talk wid Jesus, makes it right."

Sarah, was a little taller than Ruth, smooth dark complexion, with a full round face. She had, a slender build, but was muscular, she lived and worked on a farm all her life, like Ruth, and was used to working hard. For town, she wore a full skirt and short, puffed sleeved shirt with a cloth band around her waist. Her hair was pulled and wound up tight under her hat, Sarah, like Ruth, also liked a wide-brimmed straw hat to keep the sun from her face. The hat she wore today for her trip to town had some dried yellow daisies held by a brilliant blue ribbon which matched her shirt; it was tied in a bow and sewn at the brim for decoration.

Sarah had a somewhat short, and no nonsense way about her, but her heart was pure gold, and her life revolved around her husband and her children, the new church they joined, and of course, the work of helping refugees from slavery.

Sarah and Ruth knew each other for a long time. They were close in age, and met as neighbours, when Sarah and Peter lived and worked on the farm next to her Uncle's near Amherstburg. Over the years, their friendship had grown.

When Martin left for his third months-long mysterious trip, Ruth's Uncle sold two of his farm tracts to Sarah and Peter, moving them next to Ruth and Martin. It was a good deal for Sarah and Peter, because they would own their own farm outright within eight years. It was also good for Ruth, because now her best friend was living next door!

"Hi Ruth!" Sarah interrupted her song as she jumped down from the buckboard, and caught Anna as she leaped into her mother's arms. "I have to go to town this morning, so I can ride Josh and Daniel to school."

Anna's chubby little baby-fat legs carried her up to the house, and she stormed through the living room into the kitchen.

"Look at Anna!" Ruth laughed as she and Sarah followed Anna into the house. "She's growing fast, and she's walking so well on her own!"

Busybody Anna headed directly for the pile of wicker baskets in the corner which Ruth used to gather eggs and vegetables. It was her favorite place to be at Ruth's house. Josh and Daniel followed slowly, as they bantered about the day ahead and meeting their friends at school. The boys were close in age, height and demeanour. They loved to fish with Josh's father Peter, by the river, and were both eager for the time when they were old enough to be active in the project of helping refugees settle in Canada.

"Do you need anything from town Ruth?"

"I'm running low on yeast, Sarah. Why don't you leave Anna to play here while you do your errands in town, and we can have tea before you go home? I'll be working inside most of the morning, Anna can help me, can't you Anna?"

Anna ignored everyone, twirling and dancing around the kitchen with one of the baskets on her head; she was lost in wicker basket heaven! Josh and Daniel laughed at Anna. "Look at her!" "She's just being silly!" "She's going to get dizzy and fall!" they said. Anna started to giggle and 'hammed it up' even more once she noticed she had an audience.

"Just you wait 'till your mother has your new baby Daniel!" Sarah laughed: "You'll be living with the same fun!" The boys both continued laughing and teasing each other.

After Sarah and the boys left, Ruth moved Anna and the baskets into what would now be her room alone. She started piling up the clothes and things Martin left behind. Some of the clothing could be used for refugees, and any special things he left behind she would save for Daniel. She just felt she had to do some organizing before the new baby arrived.

He listened to the steady clump of his horse's hooves as they eased down the road towards the Chippewa Band's property. Peter Berry was thinking about the first conversation he had with Ruth's Uncle Samuel about their farm.

"I want this to be a good deal for you," Samuel said "but I also need someone to watch over my niece. I can't put my finger on it, but that man, Martin is just not trustworthy. As well, I don't like the way he treats you coloured people, or the Chippewa People who were living in this land first. "As far as the rest of the world is concerned, I am holding the mortgage on your land, just so it doesn't seem I'm giving you too good a deal. In truth I'm having the papers drawn up so that I'm selling you the two tracks of land for one dollar."

Samuel's long-time trusted lawyer, Thomas Manning saw them pass the dollar between hands, and they signed the secret deal that evening. From then on, the farm really belonged to Peter. Samuel swore him to secrecy, Peter hasn't even told Sarah. He's glad Sarah and Ruth are such good friends, because that way, Sarah willingly helps him carry out the task he promised Samuel.

"The only thing I ask for in return is to keep an eye on the comings and goings at my niece's place, and let me know if there's any problem with Martin." Samuel Patterson said.

Now Martin left again, and Peter would have to let Samuel know. Peter would explain to him that Sarah was going over there today to check on Ruth and Daniel.

Peter's background was in carpentry; on the farm where he and Sarah met, and later married, he was considered a valued worker. He liked his new farm, which was full of trees and brush, and therefore supplied lots of materials for building. In his spare time, he enjoyed making all the furniture for their new home.

As well as making his own furniture, he and another local farmer with extra trees on his land have been building special wagons. These wagons were fitted with secret compartments for hiding people to carry some of the refugees inland.

Peter was tall and had a strong build, with a dark complexion, and a square face; he was blessed with a steady and strong character. Right now, he had a worried face; he wanted to see if the Band sentries noticed Martin travelling last night. More importantly, would they have someone to guide the new arrivals further inland to Chatham, in Kent County tomorrow morning?

When he arrived at the Band's property Peter noticed things were not normal today. This was a permanent settlement for the people. He noticed there was more of a hurried purpose to the movements and people rushed between their, single-family frame houses. They seemed to be carrying messages between families. There was worry in their eyes, as they went about their business.

Siwili was polite, as always, to Peter. He even seemed to welcome the opportunity to send young Apenimon (Worthy of Trust), his son, to guide and help the new couple move inland to Chatham. He even offered one of the Band horses to drive the wagon Peter had arranged for them, he said: "It is a gift for the new people."

Siwili was older than Peter, about the age of Samuel Patterson. His straight black hair, which was not braided today, flowed gently in the easy breeze under the leather headband tied at the side above his left ear. His hair was starting to show a few grey strands; his face, with its dark, deep-set eyes, and strong square jaw, showed more lines of worry than usual. He was as tall as Peter, and his build was athletic.

Siwili and the other people in the Band farmed in the summer, trapped in the winter, and traded furs and handicrafts with local merchants. He had been doing business with Samuel for many years.

The Band community was located a few kilometers downstream from the Sandwich Settlement. The single–family dwellings stood on one side of the settlement and on the other side stood a longhouse. The longhouse was erected to use for political and ceremonial meetings.

The Jesuits came first to the area and ministered to the local native people long before the English came. Ruth Logan, known to them through her Uncle and Aunt, was also friends with the Chippewa People. Ruth and her Aunt Elizabeth, and now Sarah, are friends with Siwili's wife, Maka (Earth), and several of the other ladies. Besides helping with the farm work, the women of the Band wove baskets, and did other handicrafts, which they sold or traded with the settlers.

The barter arrangement ran rampant among all the close neighbours, trading back and forth as neighbours do.

It was nearing time for the noon meal when Sarah finished her errands and arrived back at Ruth's house. During the morning Ruth and Anna were very busy for a while, on their own separate projects.

Ruth cleared out Martin's things; there didn't seem to be anything of value to pass on to Daniel. She straightened and prepared her room for her and the new baby. Little Anna busied herself with her mysterious task of moving baskets around.

Soon, they both tired, and took a nap on Ruth's bed. By the time Sarah came back, Anna was back on the kitchen floor with the baskets, and Ruth had the kettle on for tea. She had also prepared some tomato vegetable soup and biscuits for the three of them.

After grace was said Sarah opened with:

"We saw Martin leave last night, are you and Daniel okay?" She looked at her old friend with inquiring eyes.

The two women had been sharing joys and sorrows for many years, praying, laughing and crying together, helping each other and working through the trials and joys of life.

"Just yelling, Daniel heard it. It makes me upset when Daniel hears us. Martin said he's not coming back this time, and I believe him. He didn't even try to say he was looking to start a new business in another place and for us to move, no excuse at all. He's never done that before."

Ruth paused, and then added. "It's an odd feeling, I don't feel as bad as I think I should; just relieved. I can finally relax and have some peace.

"At least now he's decided to leave for good, he can't hinder the work we need to do here for the refugees. He always said he was travelling to find a better place for us somewhere else, but never said what he was planning to do, or where he was planning to take us. I don't want to live anywhere but here, this is my home, with my family and friends. Besides, there is so much work to do here."

"Did he say anything at all about where he was going this time?" said Sarah.

"No, he never does," Ruth had a faraway look in her eye, as she answered. "The trips are all so mysterious; it makes me wonder if he's actively causing or planning trouble somewhere. He's so against the work we do here to help the refugees."

Her attention returned to Sarah as she added: "At least, if he's really gone, I won't have to think about him anymore."

"Don't worry about when the baby comes, Ruth." encouraged Sarah, "All of us neighbours will band together and take care of you and Daniel, and the new little one! Maybe you'll have a daughter too, and she can play with Anna."

"A girl would be fun! Thank you Sarah, it's comforting to have such a good friend, and lots of loving neighbours." She smiled and started to muse about the thought of her new baby. "It would be fun to have a daughter to dress up in lace."

"All gone!" Piped in Anna

"You have more of your biscuit to eat, Anna" Sarah pointed out to her.

"No — pay, pay more" replied Anna

"Play, you mean to say play." corrected Sarah.

"Oh Sarah, Anna's been so busy moving the baskets around this morning, I hope I can find all of them when you're gone!" Ruth laughed. "Having her here today was good practice for when this little one comes." She said caressing her stomach.

"Anna sure is a busy one! She keeps me going just to keep up with her! Seriously though, I have to tell you Peter went to the Band today about the new people, who have to move inland. But he is also going to see your Auntie and Uncle. He will tell them Martin's left again. I'm just warning you, they might be by soon to check on you and Daniel."

"Thanks for telling me, I'm so glad Peter will let them know. I was wondering how I would get word to them." Ruth answered. "Martin takes our horse when he leaves. I know my Auntie and Uncle are concerned about what happens with us, they have been such a source of strength all my life. Other than day-to-day things right now, I don't have much of a plan for our future yet." Ruth paused, and then added ruefully. "I do wish, however, I'd made a better choice for a husband."

✦

The two worried men walked and talked a long time. Peter and Siwili first got to really know each other when Sarah and Peter were living in Ruth's bunkhouse while their own home was being built. A mutual respect and trust relationship was developing between them. After today's initial conversation, they brought a few Band members along on a trip near Amherstburg.

Taima (Thunder), one of the younger band members, was sent ahead to bring Samuel Patterson to meet them on their errand. After much discussion and planning, the men made their final decision.

The last stop Peter had to make today was to see John Hubbs, the pastor of the newly organized Sandwich First Baptist Church. Pastor Hubbs is a former refugee who made the crossing of the Detroit River over twenty years ago. When he settled in Sandwich Town, he met and married a local woman, and they have two sons. They host the Sunday meetings at their farm house for fellow worshippers.

"Tomorrow morning, hide the new arrivals in our wagon, and bring them down to the Band. Siwili said he would have his son Apenimon take them to Chatham." Peter told the Pastor.

Peter was gone the whole day and finally, finished all his errands. It was late when Sarah heard the clip clop of his horse's hooves coming slowly down the lane toward their house. She met him in the barn when he was bedding his horse down.

"I kept some stew hot for you, just in case you are hungry." Sarah told him.

"Thanks honey, Maka cooked for me and I ate with the family, but it's a long ride from the Band, I think I will have some of your stew.

"Siwili said his son can take the new folks up Chatham way tomorrow morning, they should be safe there. I stopped off at Pastor Hubbs' house and told him he could take them to the Band in a wagon where Apenimon will bring them to safety. Siwili even offered one of the Band horses to pull the wagon.

"Oh yes, I saw Samuel, and told him about Martin. He and Elizabeth will be checking on Ruth and Daniel this weekend.

"At the Band, last night's sentry did see Martin Logan heading east — said he was travelling fast and looked very determined."

The three men had decided just how many details to tell others.

"Ruth and Daniel seemed okay today." Sarah added as they walked hand in hand up to the house. "Ruth was busy in the house and Daniel seems to be taking it all in stride. Ruth said Martin was very angry last night and told her he will not be coming back this time. She said Martin yelled, but didn't hurt them."

Peter put his arm around Sarah's shoulder as they walked back to the house. He wondered though; just how long will this secret stay hidden?

The next morning at the break of dawn, out of sight from the main road, at the back of his property, Rev. John Hubbs showed the new arrivals the secret compartment in the bottom of the wagon and they climbed in for the last leg of their long journey. He then loaded his 'stores' and his saddle on top of the compartment and drove the wagon to the Band's property. When they reached the settlement, away from the main road, the new people got out of the secret compartment to stretch their legs before the next leg of their trip.

Apenimon was anxious to start this trip and in a very good mood. He was in his early thirties and had a wife and two young sons, one eight, and another four years old, who were all on hand to say farewell to the travellers. Apenimon was tall and strong like his father, who was also on hand for the send-off.

Welcome was given to the new arrivals, and pleasantries were exchanged by Apenimon, Siwili and Rev. Hubbs. Then Rev Hubbs got his saddle from the wagon, and prepared his horse for the ride home. Apenimon left shortly after for his errand in Chatham with the new people back in the compartment of the wagon, the new horse hitched to the wagon, and his own horse trailing it.

Rev. Hubbs stayed long enough to see Apenimon and the new arrivals well on their way. He thanked Siwili for his dedication to the cause, and left for home.

About two weeks later, Siwili and Taima arrived at Ruth's farm with two young horses. Taima, in his late teens was being given a new responsibility by the Band. He would be expected to carry out this long-term responsibility for several years until Daniel was old enough to do it himself.

What wasn't told to Ruth was that her Uncle Samuel bought the horses from the Band. He had also made a financial arrangement with the Band people to help with the horses and farm and to help Peter keep an eye on her and her children. This was the first part of the long term goal the men had planned for Ruth and her family. The second part of the plan involved all of Sandwich, Amherstburg and Essex County.

"Hi Siwili, Taima; what brings you here today?"

"Hello, Ruth; we wanted to bring you these two horses, you will need transportation with the new baby coming and Martin gone again. Taima here has offered to help with the horses until Daniel is old enough to handle them by himself. He will train them for the buckboard and riding."

"Oh, my!" Ruth said, astonished,

"They're two years old, and ready to start working for you."

When Taima came back later that day after Daniel was home from school, he started showing Daniel the job of training and caring for the horses.

Daniel was excited! Taima was a 'big guy' and it would be fun to work along with him, just like having an older brother! The young man and the young boy would form an enduring friendship.

Ruth was still trying to figure the generous gesture out in her head.

Strange.

June, 1840:
CHAPTER 1

Ruth surveyed the final job in her kitchen with gratitude and amazement. Peter, Scott MacMillan, the local blacksmith, and Gordon Burke, a neighbouring farmer, had just added two bedrooms to her house, totalling four, and enlarged her kitchen as well.

Uncle Samuel bought a new, bigger stove, so she could cook for several people at a time. Peter and Gordon made her a bigger table and several chairs to surround it. Gordon had returned to his farm, and his family before Ruth's arrival, but Peter and Scott were there to see her reaction to the unveiling.

"Oh Peter and Scott thank you, this is such a wonderfully grand table. You two and Gordon did an excellent job on my house!" She said, running her hand across the table top and envisioning the table filled with food she had made in her new kitchen and the chairs filled with happy visitors.

Uncle Samuel and Aunt Elizabeth had just returned Ruth and Sammy, Uncle Samuel's namesake, who was now almost two years old to their home after three weeks of renovations were finished. Little Sammy, delighted himself in exploring every inch of the new rooms. Daniel, now nine, stayed at the Berry's house during the renovations, and Daniel and Josh were learning while working along with the men. The boys beamed with pride at the sight of Ruth and Sammy's reactions to their new and improved home.

"This way, we can stay with you overnight if the need arises, and now the boys can each have their own room." Uncle Samuel said. "The men want to get started on fixing up your bunkhouse and barn for the refugees who seem to be coming more regularly through here from the

South. Now your home can be another safe place to hide people, while we arrange to move those who need to go inland.

"This is wonderful." Ruth exclaimed. "With the work you have done in my kitchen, there will be lots of room to prepare the extra meals I'll be making."

Scott added. "Ruth, we've been talking about adding some secret places to your barn. We want to enlarge your bunkhouse, so it meets the barn. Then build a secret doorway from the bunkhouse into the barn. As well, we want to enlarge the barn big enough to park a whole wagon inside, that way, no one can see us when we load people to hide in the wagon."

"Right," Peter added, "As well, we need to build a secret spot in your hay loft, where we can safely hide people if catchers start to look around the bunkhouse."

"Good idea." Ruth answered, "If we are going to get really involved with this project, we might as well do a good job, and take the challenge seriously."

"I agree with them, they have been working hard, and planning for a smooth operation as far as helping people get to safety." Uncle Samuel added. "Auntie and I have to be getting back home so we will leave you for now. God bless you and keep you until we meet again!"

When the hugs and kisses were done, and things calmed down and after all the company left, Ruth took the opportunity to really explore her new rooms and especially the kitchen. The new bedrooms still needed beds and furniture. Uncle Samuel and Auntie Elizabeth wouldn't be able to stay until the rooms were ready.

Ruth decided to go to town the next morning with Daniel and Sammy to get a few provisions. She wanted to order material for bedding, and other things she needed for the new rooms. She would also need to buy the things needed once the bunkhouse was finished.

When morning came, Ruth prepared for the trip to town, but Daniel didn't want to go.

"Josh and I want to go fishing today." He said. "We've been working real hard on the house, and we'd like to take some time for fun! Besides, Momma, we can bring home fish for supper tonight."

"Okay." Ruth said. "You and Josh deserve a good time, because of all your hard work. I'll go alone with Sammy, and see you later when you and Josh are done fishing. I'll be looking forward to fish for the evening meal tonight!"

Under The North Star

The next morning Ruth and Sammy arrived at the General Store in town; she parked her wagon in the front and tied the horse to the hitching post. The General Store was run by Seamus and Mary Anne Murphy. They moved here from Toronto many years ago, when their children were young and started up their store right away. Seamus and Mary Anne are abolitionists, and actively participate in the project of helping refugees.

Mary Anne's face brightened when Ruth and Sammy entered her store. "Hi Ruth!" She came around the counter and bent down to Sammy's level and said. "Hi Sammy, it's good to see you." Looking up to Ruth she said. "How is all the work going on your house?"

"I think they're done with the house, but they still have to work on the bunkhouse and the barn." Ruth answered. "Now if the weather turns, or something is going on in town, Uncle Samuel and Auntie Elizabeth won't have to come in town or travel all the way home, they can stay with me."

"We've been waiting for you." Mary Anne answered, her kindly face showed concern for Ruth. "Philip, the new Postmaster was in here last week, and said when you came to the shop, to have you go to see him, you have a letter. I hope it's nothing to worry about."

"Oh, I wonder what the letter is about." She paused, and then added. "I'll go there later. I'd like to look at your yard goods right now. I have to make bedding for those new beds I have to buy, and curtains for all my new windows!"

Ruth picked out the material she needed, and ordered the things which weren't in stock. As Ruth gathered her money together for all her purchases, Mary Anne presented Sammy with a peppermint stick:

"What a good boy you have been this morning Sammy. You have been so patient while your mother was doing her shopping"

"Tank 'oo' Mrs. Muffy." Sammy answered, while flashing his shy little smile.

Ruth and Mary Anne smiled at him as he shoved the candy stick in his mouth. Seamus then loaded the order on her buckboard along with some food and other supplies she ordered from her list.

"This should keep you busy," he said smiling.

Her next stop was across the street to the Post Office to see who was writing a letter to her. Maybe Martin had contacted her about

3

something. She stood up straight, and steeled herself for whatever the news was. This letter came just as she was starting to feel comfortable planning for herself and her sons, and not worry about what he thought.

Seamus put his arm around Mary Anne's shoulder as they stood at the door to their shop and watched Ruth and Sammy make their way across the street. Ruth held one of Sammy's hands as he held the peppermint stick in his mouth with the other. Once across the street, Ruth and Sammy then slowly climbed up the stairs of the Sandwich Post Office.

"Hi Philip, I hear you have something for me." She said to the Postmaster.

"Hi Ruth, how's the house coming?" He said.

"It's getting done!"

"Here's the letter, but it's not for you, I didn't know what to do about it. Is Martin Logan your husband?" Philip handed the letter to Ruth, and watched the reaction on her face as she read the envelope.

The letter was addressed to Martin Logan, not Ruth. The Postmark said it was written from London in Middlesex County, not Toronto, and she did not recognize the sender's name. She was confused, and told herself: "I don't want to have any more to do with that man. This can't be good news, and can't be anything I want to deal with."

Ruth slid the unopened letter back over the counter top to him and said:

"Philip, I don't know where Martin is. He never told me where he was going. Just write on the envelope **'return to sender address not known'**. I really don't want anything to do with his affairs."

"I will Ruth, but are you okay?" Philip worried. "I didn't mean to upset you. I just didn't know what to do about the letter."

"I'll be okay Philip. I was surprised to hear about him. He said he was never coming back, and I would never hear from him again. I believed him."

Her mood brightened. "My home is almost all done, and I am looking forward to filling the new rooms with joy and laughter! I have lots to think about without worrying about what Martin is doing!" She paused and added thoughtfully. "Let's just keep this between you and me, okay?"

"No problem Ruth, I'll do what you asked with the letter, and not say a word to anyone." Philip replied.

On the way home, Ruth wondered if she should tell someone about the letter, but decided she wouldn't. Mostly because she didn't want to think about how whatever Martin was doing might affect her. On

Monday Peter, Gordon and Scott would start working on the bunkhouse and barn. This would be a busy summer.

※

No one was home when Ruth returned. She didn't really expect Daniel to be back before her. The boys' favorite fishing spot was on Peter and Sarah's land. There was a little cove on the river front with a narrow opening which was sheltered by bush on the shore, away from the main stream of the river where their farm fronted. It was private and out of clear sight from the river, seemed to be a good place to catch fish, and the boys loved going there.

At first, Peter would take them, and later they would go with Taima and his brother Kajika (Walks Without Sound), but now the boys were bigger, and they were allowed to go fishing alone. Now, when they went, when they were able, it was an all day trip.

While putting some of the food things away in the kitchen, she noticed when Daniel left he had packed cheese and bread for his lunch. She smiled as she thought the boys would probably come back with plenty of fish for supper tonight. They usually went to Josh's house first to drop off the fishing rods. If Sarah noticed there were extra fish, she would see to it they delivered some to the Burke's, Gordon and his family, their farm was on the other side of Ruth's.

※

At the cove on Peter and Sarah's land the boys were having good luck catching fish, and relaxing. Locally, the place was called Berry's Cove, only a few select people knew about this favorite spot on Peter's land. It also served as a sheltered place for rowboats to land on the nights when refugees came.

Early this afternoon, Josh and Daniel were surprised by the daylight arrival of a rowboat entering into the cove where they fished.

"Oh no, Josh, a boat is coming, and in the daytime!" Daniel exclaimed. The boys knew it was dangerous to cross in daylight.

When Josh saw the boat coming, he told Daniel. "Go get my Poppa, Daniel, he usually tells me if people are coming; tell him about the boat."

"Okay" Daniel replied as he ran off towards the Berry house.

Soon, just before the rowboat landed, Peter was standing alone at the cove with his rifle. He had sent the boys back to the house with the fish and orders go to town and bring Scott MacMillan back here as soon as possible.

There were four black people in the boat, Peter recognized the man rowing, as one of the conductors from the movement in Detroit.

"Oh Joseph, it's you! You didn't signal! Why are you coming now? You know it's not safe to land when it's this light outside!" Peter exclaimed. "You're just lucky it was my boy and his friend who were here today fishing."

"I know Peter," The conductor said. "I'm sorry I didn't signal my arrival, but I had to take the chance. Things are jumping over in Detroit, I'm in danger. The wrong people know what I've been doing. My family and I have come to stay over here!"

A worried Peter looked at Joseph and his family, he met Joseph's wife Mary, once, but he didn't know their two sons. Immediately, he wished he, Gordon and Scott had the bunkhouse and barn finished at Ruth's farm. Peter helped Joseph with the unloading his family from the boat. Joseph's older son took one of his mother's arms from the inside and Joseph, first on the shore, took her other hand to help her step out, while the younger son stood behind to offset the balance in the boat.

When the offloading was completed Peter sent mother and sons, carrying the few belongings they were able to bring with them up to the house. As the two men pulled the boat into the nearby brush to hide it, Peter said to Joseph:

"I think you should at least have a meal here. We'll find a place for you to stay tonight, until we can make plans for you and your family for a safer place to stay inland."

When they had the boat well hidden, the men went to join their families at Peter's farmhouse. In the house they saw, Mary assisting Sarah with a quick supper including the fish the boys caught. Anna, who was now four years old, was busy setting places for everyone at their large kitchen table.

Sarah took Peter aside and said quietly: "Josh and Daniel went together to get Scott."

"Good, we weren't expecting people today and we need to make plans quickly to hide them until we can move them away from the river." Peter answered quietly to Sarah.

Joseph formally introduced his family to Peter, Sarah, and Anna: "Peter, you remember my wife, Mary; these are my sons, Joseph Junior, JJ for short, and Jake. We're grateful for your help today, I've helped many people, and now the wrong people have learned about me and what I've been doing it's no longer safe for me or my family in Detroit."

Sarah had them all sit at the table and after they thanked the Lord for the safety thus far, and especially for the generous portions of fish the boys provided, they shared the hasty meal.

Josh and Daniel rode double on one of Peter's horses to the blacksmith's shop, hitched it at the post in front, and ran up to the storefront. The boys were excited, but experienced enough with what was going on to be very worried. They didn't know what to expect when they got back to the Berry's house. If the wrong someone had seen the family cross the river, there might be someone else following them and causing trouble at Josh's home.

Bursting in the door, Josh blurted out breathlessly: "Mr. MacMillan, my Poppa sent us to tell you some refugees just came over by boat, and he needs you at my house now. He said the people have to be moved fast."

"Now? It's still light!" Scott exclaimed, and then to his father he asked: "Poppa, can you mind the shop alone for now?"

"Aye son, do what must be done." The senior Mr. MacMillan replied.

"Boys, I have a wagon in the back of the shop Gordon delivered yesterday, let me hook it up and we can leave together. Does your Poppa know where the people can go for tonight Josh?"

"I don't think so Mr. MacMillan, we didn't expect anyone today." Replied Josh.

The boys tied their horse to the back of the wagon and climbed up front with Scott, who drove quickly towards Peter's house. When they were coming up to pass Ruth's farm, Scott let Daniel off at the roadway to the farm.

"Tell your mother what's going on, we may have to bring the new people here for safety to stay in your bunkhouse."

"Okay Mr. MacMillan," Daniel smiled at him as he added. "I'll tell her, but I think she and Sammy might miss the fish we caught for supper tonight!"

A little over an hour later, Scott returned to Ruth's farm with Joseph and his family. Ruth helped him settle the new family in her bunkhouse for the night.

After they left Joseph and his family alone to settle in, Scott said to Ruth: "It's too bad we haven't had time to fix up this old bunkhouse, Peter and I wanted to make some repairs to the building as well as enlarge the place so more people can stay at once."

"Tell me about the new people Scott, they look like a family."

"Yes they are. Peter knows the father; the family are very upset because they had to leave behind all their extended family and friends. His oldest son, J.J. especially because he had to leave his girlfriend."

"That's so sad; I know it's the same with everyone who makes the trip over here. I'm glad at least you, Gordon and Peter were able to fix my kitchen up so I can cook for this new family tomorrow morning! You men did a wonderful job."

She paused as she thought about all he, Peter and Gordon had been doing for her over the years.

"Did you eat yet? I had Daniel kill a chicken for our supper, since I was sure the fish were needed at the Berry's house."

"Thanks Ruth, I appreciate your asking, but I know my father is cooking for me tonight. I'll be back in the morning to help move Joseph and his family further inland. He says he doesn't want to go too far away, because he knows several people who stayed in Essex County. I'm going to leave the wagon here, and just take my horse for tonight."

"Of course Scott, no problem, I'll see you in the morning. Have a good night, and pass my greetings on to your father." Ruth gently leaned on the inside of her front door and sighed after she closed it behind him, such a good and kind man. Sometimes, adult male company would be nice. She sighed again.

Scott left for home, the horse and rider became one as his tall, muscular form slowly swayed with the graceful movement of the horse. Scott ran a hand through the short, chestnut brown curls in his hair.

"Ruth has a kind heart and is a nice lady." He thought as he mulled over his few choices of available women in Town. "Too bad she's a married woman."

The next morning, things went according to plan as far as moving Joseph's family in the care of more friends of the movement further inland, but still in Essex County. Peter and Scott drove the special wagon to some of Joseph's friends in the county near the Puce River. They were able to return by late afternoon.

For Ruth, it was a quiet but busy weekend; she tackled the job of catching up on her chores around the house and farm. Things sure did pile up while she was away.

Taima showed up later in the morning to help and guide Daniel with his regular work around the farm. They took care of feeding and caring for the two horses, three cows and the chickens.

Taima and Daniel had become very close friends over the years. Sometimes, when they had time, Taima would bring his younger brother, Kajika and fish with Josh and Daniel at their favorite spot. He also showed them how to find signs in the woods and how to track animals.

Ruth is grateful for his unwavering devotion to the horses and his wonderful influence on Daniel.

Sammy shadowed Taima and Daniel for a while, and then started following Ruth. The planting on the farm was done in the early spring. When the bunkhouse was finished, Ruth could again hire occasional summer help on the farm. Now, with the added space and the new larger table they were building in the main room of the bunkhouse, it would be more comfortable.

On Sunday, Ruth and her family worshipped at Sandwich Methodist church in town. The Pastor at Sandwich was Gordon's father, Pastor Michael Burke. He, his sons and some of the local members built the church on part of the Burke property nearest to the edge of town. It was a wooden building, but made with loving and faithful devotion. Scott and his father worshipped there also.

Ruth and her family happily rejoined the church family after a few weeks away. She and Sammy had been worshipping in Amherstburg and Daniel at Sandwich First Baptist services with the Berry family.

During today's service she privately rejoiced in the progress made on the house, and the plans for the future work. She prayed all the work to be done would go well, and there would be health and safety for all who worked on the project. She prayed for the health and safety of her and her sons and the crops that were germinating. As always, she prayed for all the refugees who would be helped this summer, and for as many summers it would take until slavery was abolished in the United States.

She also made a special prayer for whatever was going on with the mysterious letter from London, and that it did not signal trouble from Martin.

On Monday, Peter, Scott and Gordon started their work on Ruth's bunkhouse and barn. Of course, their loyal 'helpers' Daniel and Josh eagerly did most of the 'running, and carrying' for the men.

The first project was to enlarge the barn, add the secret room, and the hiding place in the hay loft. Since the days were clear, and warm, the animals would be moved outside each day while the work was being done.

Ruth had Sammy working in a small garden at the side of the house, away from the main work on the barn, she asked him to dig weeds to prepare for flowers to come.

In the house, Ruth continued with preparations for the new rooms. She occasionally checked on Sammy's progress as she started her work. She needed new sheets and pillow cases, and planned for the curtains for the windows in the two new rooms and the extra windows in the larger kitchen. On Saturday when she was in the store, Mary Anne told her the material for the curtains would take at least a month to arrive.

Presently, Ruth heard the sounds of a buckboard coming down the lane, but didn't pay attention to it. Since there was so much work going on outside, she figured someone was coming to help or deliver materials. Loud knocking called her to the kitchen door where she found a wide-eyed Sarah and Anna. Sarah exclaimed:

"Ruth, some white men from Detroit are rowing up and down on this side of the river and staring at the shore. I'm afraid they will find our cove."

Peter and Ruth's farmhouse was on a rise, and from the house, they could see the main stream of the river over their cove.

"They are in a large rowboat and I'm afraid they are looking for the rowboat Joseph used to come over. I don't feel safe."

"Oh no!" Ruth exclaimed. She then turned to Anna. "Anna, will you please help Sammy in the side garden for a while so your mother and I can talk to your Poppa and the other men?" Ruth guided Anna, towards the place where she had Sammy working, while Sarah went directly to talk to the men.

"Okay Auntie Ruth, how can I help?" Anna realized she was being given some responsibility and relished the honour.

"We are just weeding now." Ruth answered as she guided the two young future farmers with the digging.

When she finally arrived at the barn, Sarah was just finishing her report to Peter and the others on what was happening at the river by her farm.

Peter, Gordon, Scott and Taima, who arrived earlier for his daily time with Daniel, jumped into action. They each grabbed their rifles and saddled their horses. They then headed towards the Berry farm by the back lane only used between the Berry's and the Logan's. They gave Josh and Daniel stern directions to 'stay here and guard their mothers and siblings'.

"Tea time," Ruth said: "We can only make some lunch and wait now."

"Right," Sarah answered, "I don't like it when the catchers take to the boats. I'm thankful they don't seem to have found our cove yet."

When the men arrived at the Berry Farm, they left their horses in Peter's barn, and quietly headed for the river bank. They didn't go near the cove, but headed to the east side of the Berry's farm, almost to Ruth's property, there the shore was more visible to the eye from the river. In this area, as with most of the shore line around here, there was a steep drop to the river.

The local men could see the large rowboat still slowly moving back and forth near the shore. There were four men in the boat and they were definitely looking for something. Fortunately, they had not yet noticed the entrance to Berry's Cove.

Gordon hollered from the shore: "What are you looking for?"

"A coloured man stole my rowboat the other day and my neighbour told me he came this way. He must have stowed it around here somewhere." A grey-haired spokesman from the boat replied.

"This is all private farm land up here, we would have known about any unexpected landings. None of us farmers around here have seen strangers." Gordon replied. "You men coming up and down this shore are worrying our wives; we have to ask you to leave our shore. Our children fish and play here and we don't want any strangers near."

"My boat must be hidden around here somewhere." The spokesman from the large rowboat answered.

"Maybe the man was just visiting and came back to your shore." Scott suggested, "In any case, we are asking you to leave our shore and not come back. We don't want any strangers lurking near our property."

"Okay." He said slowly. "We'll leave for now." With that, the boat slowly headed away from Canadian soil.

The four local men stayed at the shore until they saw the boat land on the other side of the river.

After waiting a while longer they left and headed for Peter's barn and their horses. A sense of uneasiness returned to Ruth's farm with them.

They would have to find some way to shelter the entrance to Berry's Cove. But how would they do it?

"The men in the boat are gone for now." Peter said. "But we have to think of a way to protect the entrance to the cove."

Sarah and Ruth had enough stew with bread and tea made for a hardy lunch for everyone. The returning men seemed to appreciate the meal. Gordon gave the blessing for the food and for the ease they had in encouraging the strangers to leave their shore.

During lunch, there was discussion around the large outside table about ways to shelter and protect the cove from unwanted visitors, but no real resolution to the problem.

After lunch and the clean-up were finished, Sarah and Anna returned home. Sammy went down for a nap, and Ruth returned to her work. The other men and Josh returned to work on the barn. When Taima finished his work with Daniel and left for home, Daniel joined the others to work on the barn.

As a result of some of the discussion at Monday's lunch, the men all took Tuesday off from working on Ruth's barn. Peter and Gordon loaded Joseph's rowboat on a wagon and took Josh, Daniel, and Gordon's son, Jacob for a ride to the county.

The idea was to return Joseph's boat to him; so he could use it to fish the local streams. If the boat was returned to Detroit, there was a risk of it being recognized. There was a risk of it being found if it stayed in Berry's Cove.

Three weeks later, the work on Ruth's barn and bunkhouse was done, and Ruth's home was ready for any new refugees who came.

Occasionally, they would see people searching up and down the river, but not near the Berry's Cove area. The residents with farms fronting on the river started keeping better watch and reporting what they saw. The locals were still praying for safety, and wondering what else they could do to shelter the cove from unwanted visitors.

October, 1843:
CHAPTER 2

"It's been five years since he left Ruthie! You have to try to file for divorce through abandonment! Uncle Samuel and I won't live forever, and we can't leave all our property to HIM!!"

Aunt Elizabeth was right. She and Uncle Samuel took Ruth in as a small child when her parents, William and Phoebe Patterson, were both killed during the War of 1812. Uncle Samuel's farm in Amherstburg was not far from Fort Malden.

Ruth's father was a soldier and she and her mother lived near the fort with him. Before his last battle, her parents had taken Ruth to safety with William's older brother, Samuel and his wife, Elizabeth. They were childless, and treasured her as a gift from God. They were both devastated when William and his wife, Phoebe were both killed in a raid on Fort Malden, but they were grateful Ruth's parents were careful enough to bring her to them for safety.

She was a light in their life, and completed their family; they felt God had given them a very special child. Elizabeth loved Ruth as a daughter, and Ruth's children as her own grandchildren.

Aunt Elizabeth's normally laughing hazel eyes were serious. At forty-eight, her dark brown hair, had not started to grey, but worry lines were beginning to appear. Today, she was dressed for town, with a brightly coloured frock, and a matching hat. As usual when they left the farm; she and Uncle Samuel dressed for travel.

After Ruth's marriage Samuel and she had talked endlessly about what to do to protect Ruth from Martin's greed and shifty behaviour. But, just before little Sammy was born, after Martin left for the last time Samuel didn't seem so worried. She didn't understand why he didn't talk about why he felt the difference. Still, Aunt Elizabeth thought safeguards had to be taken to protect Ruth in case Martin ever returned.

Sammy, Uncle Samuel's namesake, now almost five years old, ran around the front yard with his new puppy. He didn't seem to care that officially, he had to share him with his older brother. Ah, but Daniel was at school now, and the — yet unnamed puppy — was all his! Ruth and Elizabeth sat on the back veranda preparing vegetables for the evening's meal while they continued their conversation.

"I know you're right Auntie," Ruth said "I just don't want you to go to all the expense, when divorce is almost impossible in Canada West — I can't get used to calling us Canada West! I remember your lawyer, Mr. Manning said how hard it is to get a divorce here the chances are slim the divorce will be granted."

"We have to try," Elizabeth said: "With the laws as they are now, as long as you're married, we can't leave anything to you, in your name. You're a married woman, and all property has to be in your husband's name. Mr. Manning is looking into it now.

We can't leave anything to that man, he could swoop in and take everything and leave nothing for you and your sons. If we leave everything to the boys, as long as they're minors, he can still, as their father take over. I'm so worried about you and the boys."

"Oh Auntie Elizabeth, if it wasn't for you and Uncle Samuel helping we'd be destitute, I love you both so much."

Ruth became suddenly quiet as she wondered to herself. "I wonder where he is and who is looking for Martin?"

There were those three letters which started coming a few years after Martin left, and came every so often to the Post Office. The letters were from an unknown person and address in London in Middlesex County.

"Why London," she thought, "he said he was from Toronto?" Each time she had Philip, the Postmaster send them back and write on the envelope '**Return to sender, address not known**'.

Ruth briefly wondered if she should have told her uncle and aunt when they came. Now that Auntie was worrying, she thought maybe she should warn them someone was looking for Martin. Sammy's voice brought her back to the present.

"Momma look at me!" Sammy ran in circles and the puppy followed him, nipping at his heels. "He's following me! He's so smart!"

The puppy was a product of questionable heritage from her aunt and uncle's farm. Samuel and Elizabeth figured he might be some protection if 'catchers' came by, or if Martin Logan decided to return.

"EEEEahhh! Look now!" Sammy demanded their attention. The paws on that black, brown and tan puppy were huge; he was going to be like his mother — about 100 pounds! He was a curious mixture; longish hair, big ears, which stood up at the back, and flopped over in the front. He was playful, and that's what counted with Ruth.

When his bark was strong, maybe he would make a stranger think. He had to learn to accept all the welcome visitors Ruth had. He had to accept the refugees, who were still coming, even more now. The bunkhouse was busy, especially in the summertime.

The Band people still came often, even now that Daniel, now twelve, was becoming more adept at handling the horses. Taima still came to help, and they also helped out with the refugees, and she thinks, to watch out for the security of Berry's Cove as well as her and her sons. She had a busy home, with her children, and all the extra people coming and going.

With Uncle Samuel, and Aunt Elizabeth's financial help, she was working the farm with extra labour coming from people who needed work. She was feeling good about helping with the refugees.

Ruth's Aunt and Uncle were also active in the project. They hid the refugees who landed in the Amherstburg area. In Amherstburg, sometimes people would come in large boats, with fifteen people at a time.

The Patterson farm house was near the water, and they built a secret place in their home for people who had to hide and move quickly inland.

In Sandwich Town, some of Ruth's neighbours, who lived further in the town, and Pastor Hubbs, who lived in the other direction from town, also had secret places in their homes. Ruth's farm was helpful because it was close to the main landing in the Sandwich area. It was sheltered, and the bunkhouse had a larger capacity than most of the other local homes. She remembered the summer when Peter, Gordon and Scott, did all the extra work on her farm. That was a busy summer, but the hard work back then made the work now easier.

"Well, Ruth," Aunt Elizabeth said, "We'll have to figure out something to protect you and the boys financially. — Sammy! How do you like the new puppy?"

"He's great Auntie! Can I name him Runner, 'cause he likes to run and follow me?"

Ruth reminded him: "Remember, Sammy; we're waiting for your brother to come home from school, and you two will agree on a name together!"

"Okaaay," He answered slowly. "I will wait for Daniel." Sammy said, resigned to his mother's wish.

Later, after he finished his business in town, Uncle Samuel stopped by the school to collect Josh and Daniel. He returned Josh to his home, and then brought Daniel home. Since Daniel also had to get his 'puppy playtime' in, they all decided a 'naming' discussion could wait until after the evening meal. Aunt Elizabeth and Uncle Samuel decided to stay overnight in the spare bedroom so they could hear the final decision.

Uncle Samuel was an impressive-looking man, tall and large-framed. He was older than his wife, fifty-five, years, and his once dark brown hair was now grey and thinning. He was a kind-hearted man, but his steel-blue eyes could laugh or stop you dead in your tracks. Today, as usual when he went to town, he dressed in a suit, dress shirt, tie and black bowler hat, but around his own farm, it was just a work shirt wide-brimmed farm hat and dungarees.

After grace was said by Uncle Samuel, they dined on venison stew. The vegetables Ruth and Aunt Elizabeth prepared this afternoon during their talk, and the venison complements of a neighbour who was able to shoot an extra deer while hunting for his own family. During the meal Uncle Samuel told news from town.

"Seamus and Mary-Ann from the general store were telling me today that Rev. Josiah Henson; remember him? He came up with his family about ten years ago through Fort Erie, and settled there. Well, you know he's been working hard for abolition in the United States with some folks from Toronto, as well as some Englishmen, and Americans.

"Rev. Henson and his group of abolitionists purchased a tract of land north of Chatham in Dawn Township. They're setting up a vocational training school for fugitive slaves. It is a working farm, but more importantly, there is a forest of black walnut trees, and they're planning to manufacture furniture!" Uncle Samuel said.

"What a great idea!" Aunt Elizabeth added. "It's a safe place far inland to send people where they can put down roots and learn to survive and get ahead in this land." A lively discussion followed.

Later, at the end of the evening meal, another lively discussion began — to name the puppy!

Sammy started: "Runner! Runner!"

"No! Daniel came back: "That's a puppy name, we need something tough for a big boy dog: Tiger!"

Finally, after much discussion, one of Daniel's ideas won out: "Shadow!"

Uncle Samuel agreed: "Okay, that's good: Shadow, he follows you guys, and it's a mysterious name too!"

Sammy agreed: "Okay I like Shadow too!"

"Here Shadow! Here Shadow!" called Sammy.

The newly named Shadow lifted his head from his slumber on the floor, and plopped it back down. The boys had completely tuckered him out! The family supposed Shadow didn't mind his new name.

That evening, after her sons went to bed, Ruth thought she had better tell her aunt and uncle about the letters that had been coming, and addressed to Martin.

"I'm sorry I didn't tell you earlier, but, I guess I just didn't want to think about dealing with him again." She said. "The letters were from London in Middlesex County. Martin said he was from Toronto, I don't remember him talking about anyone from London. The times he left, he never said where he was going or who he was dealing with."

"It's too bad you didn't record the address. But don't worry about it now." Uncle Samuel said. "I want you to tell us right away if you hear again. Don't send the letter back next time, let us try to contact them, maybe we can find out what he's been doing."

They all turned in after that, Ruth feeling better that she had told them, and Samuel and Elizabeth, given something more to worry about.

The next morning was Saturday and there was no school for the older boys, Peter came by early and met Shadow for the first time. As he dismounted his horse Peter was greeted with yapps and jumping up on his legs.

Uncle Samuel and Ruth met him at the hitching post near the front door.

"Off Shadow!" Ruth ordered; not much reaction from Shadow until she pulled him off and ordered again. "Sorry Peter, he has much to learn!"

Peter's mood was serious. "We've just received a message that three men arrived in Detroit, and will be brought here by rowboat late tonight. They're being chased hard and can only stay one night in your bunkhouse. We will have to slip them out by wagon from your barn first thing tomorrow morning for safer grounds."

"No problem." Ruth said. "But I don't have a wagon in my barn right now, they haven't brought one back from last time."

"Gordon has one that was brought back to be repaired from the last trip; it is all fixed up, and he will be bringing it over this afternoon. He and Jackson will be staying here to keep an eye on your farm in case the 'chasers' are closer than we think."

Peter crouched down and started playing with Shadow. "He's a cute dog, is he one of yours Samuel? Josh and Anna are excited about the puppy you and Elizabeth brought them yesterday! We called ours Chance, what is this guy's name?"

"Yes, he's one of ours, Daniel and Sammy named him Shadow." He said, "I'm glad Josh and Anna like Chance!"

"I think if this keeps up you're going to run out of people who want dogs!" Ruth added: "He seems to be friendly. By the way, Uncle Samuel, did you tell Peter about the new place in Dawn Township?"

"What place in Dawn Township?" said Peter.

"It's a vocational school that's been started by Rev. Henson. Remember when we were talking about him and the abolitionists? There is a forest of Black Walnut trees on the land they bought for the school up there. The idea is to teach the refugees' woodwork and other professions.

"Seamus and Mary Ann at the store told me about it, maybe they can tell you more." Uncle Samuel said.

While he was talking, Uncle Samuel slowly led Peter away from Ruth's range of hearing. Ruth played with Shadow while they walked and talked. Quietly, Uncle Samuel filled Peter in about the letters for Martin from London.

"Did she say anything to you or Sarah?" He asked Peter.

"No." Peter answered. "I haven't heard anything! I'll ask Sarah; in case Ruth said something and Sarah kept a secret. But I don't think Sarah would have kept that secret, since she knows I'm concerned about Ruth's safety."

"We knew there was a possibility of someone looking for him." Samuel said. "Only the Band people, you and I know anything. We just have to stay together on this."

"I agree, Samuel, we don't need anyone making up a story to fit their own agenda." Peter answered. In a louder voice so that Ruth could ear, Peter said as he mounted his horse to leave: 'I'm going to ask at the store, thanks for telling me, Samuel."

Shortly after Peter left, Ruth and her family gathered to say good bye to Samuel and Elizabeth.

"Now Ruth, I want you to remember what we were talking about yesterday, and think about what I said, remember to tell us the moment you receive another letter!" Aunt Elizabeth whispered to Ruth. In a more public voice she added. "Even though, with the new arrivals coming tonight I want you to be careful, we're glad there are so many people to help here with the project. But we always worry anyway. God bless."

"God bless, and have a safe journey home." Ruth replied, as Daniel, Sammy and she waved at the only family she knew. Ruth thought about how she loved her life here, with her children. She always felt a little sad when her dear Aunt and Uncle left for home. Daniel held Shadow in his arms as the puppy wiggled to lick his face!

Uncle Samuel and Aunt Elizabeth decided to take a detour before they returned to their farm and the work there. At the end of Ruth's laneway, Uncle Samuel turned the horses towards Sandwich Town again to tell Sheriff Pollard about Ruth's letters.

"I'm thinking if someone is looking for Martin, there should be someone on hand to help Ruth with any trouble that might happen because of Martin's absence." Samuel said.

Sheriff Richard Pollard is the part-time Sheriff as well as the Priest of St. John's Anglican Church. The Sheriff is very active, and keeps in touch with all the local merchants and clergy to better serve his community.

After leaving the seminary, Richard emigrated from England about ten years ago, and came directly to Windsor to meet up with one of his childhood friends who settled here. The two friends renewed their friendship, and now his friend is a farmer living in the county. Richard is a serious-minded person with a gentle heart, and more importantly, he is also a friend of the refugees, and the people who help them.

"Could be relatives of his," the Sheriff started, "maybe he didn't tell his family where he was going, or that he left here at all. It could be an innocent request for information."

"I hope you're right" Samuel continued, "but I just want to be careful, what with Martin's sneaky comings and goings, and his thoughts on the refugees and the native people. It could be his family, or whoever is looking for him has the same opinions as his. It would be dangerous for Ruth and the children to have those kinds of people around here. I'd appreciate it if you would just watch out for her and the boys."

"No problem Samuel, over the years Ruth and her boys have become part of the family around here."

✦

Later in the afternoon Gordon brought the wagon to the farm, and parked it in Ruth's barn. The doors to Ruth's barn were always kept closed to keep the wagons, if they were there, out of sight.

Late that night after her sons had gone to bed; Ruth put her knitting down to answer a knock at the back door. A dark-skinned man, about forty-five or fifty years old faced her in the window. She recognized him as a man called Jackson. He was one of the newer refugees, who lived

19

and worked on a neighbouring farm. His face was serious. When she opened the door he said.

"We need you in the bunkhouse."

Ruth grabbed her shawl from the hook by the door and followed him. The nights were getting cooler, it was October already; past the harvest.

When they arrived at the bunkhouse, she saw the new refugees sitting on three of the bunks, but they were in sad shape. Their clothes were tattered and they were gaunt and shaking in the cool night air. They were full of scratches, she supposed from travelling and hiding in the woods along the way. Their faces each registered only, pain and exhaustion. She didn't see Gordon. 'It must be Gordon's turn to be on watch.' She thought.

"Peter's gone fo' mo' fi'wood fo' the stove, but they needs food and clean clothes." Jackson said simply. "We can't move dem out tomorrow monin', they jus' too weak. We haf to risk lettin' dem stay here longer."

"Okay." She said quietly to Jackson. To the new refugees, Ruth said: "Welcome to Canada! I have stew cooking on the stove, give me some time, and then send someone out to help me carry the food here. Jackson will start heating some well water on the stove in here. There are some clean mended clothes, a tub, soap and towels. They are in the small room in the barn off the bunkhouse door."

Jackson and Peter helped the three refugees with a bath and clean, warm and dry clothes while Ruth cooked yet another midnight meal. Later, when Peter came to help carry the food back to the bunkhouse, he repeated what Jackson said.

"Even though it is risky, we have to give them one or two days to recover their strength before we move them inland. I can arrange for some men to appear to be working on your farm and ours, they'll keep an eye out for anything different going on."

"Its October now Peter, the harvest is in, any people watching will have to be hidden from sight." Ruth worried.

The new men looked more comfortable when Ruth and Peter arrived with the food, and they thanked her as they eagerly dug into the hot meal at the large table Peter and Gordon made when they fixed up the bunkhouse.

Ruth left the men with Peter and Jackson to welcome them. She knew Jackson would have something to eat then relieve Gordon, who would take his meal in the bunkhouse and spend the night with the new men only then, would Peter head for home.

Under The North Star

Early Sunday morning, the residents of Sandwich and the nearby farming community were getting ready for church, each preparing to go to their own House of Worship. There was Assumption Roman Catholic Church, the first church organized in the area by the Jesuits, St. John's Anglican Church, and Sandwich Methodist Church, were started with the arrival of the English, and the newly formed Sandwich First Baptist Church.

Sandwich First Baptist was started by refugees who came from the South, and some of the local population, including Peter and Sarah and their family, added to their numbers. The wooden structure which had been built a few years ago, when their numbers outgrew meetings in the pastor's farmhouse, served the growing congregation well. The church also had a secret place in the sanctuary where, if slave 'catchers' came, new people who were worshipping could quickly hide.

Scott MacMillan, the local blacksmith who had been helping with the renovations on Ruth's house, barn and bunkhouse, was just finishing breakfast with his father at the kitchen table in their living area at the back of the shop. Scott started working in the family business with his father when he was still in school.

Angus, the elder MacMillan, and his wife, Mary emigrated from Scotland when Scott was very young. Eventually they settled here in Sandwich when it was not much more than the farms. Angus started his business here, and is doing well. He has let Scott take over, but still has his active hand in the shop when he is needed. Mary passed away a few years ago, from a respiratory illness which went through the community. Now it is just the two men running the business and their home.

The men were just clearing away remnants from their meal; when suddenly they heard a loud banging at their business door. When Scott opened the door he was confronted with several angry men, who demanded to be heard. The five men were armed with guns, and accompanied by hunting dogs. Two men had dismounted their horses to confront the blacksmith at his door.

"Whar' you people keepin' those lazy slaves — our prop'ty — who passed this way las' night?" The apparent leader demanded.

"This is Canada, we have no slavery. If some people came through here, they are free now." Scott calmly answered him.

"We'll fine our prop'ty on our own!" The other spat the words back to Scott. They jumped back on their horses and all stormed off, the dogs running alongside, baying, ready for the chase.

Scott told his father, "You go and tell Sheriff Pollard at St. John's Church, and I'll tell Seamus, at the store, and then Pastor Hubbs at Sandwich Baptist. We have to warn people those men are about here."

"Some people travelled here last night son?" Angus asked.

"Aye Poppa, Seamus told me three men were arriving here last night. They were being taken to Ruth's bunkhouse." Scott answered. "We'd better get moving now."

"Aye son, I'm ready."

Scott pulled up on the reigns of his horse in front of the General Store and jumped off as he hollered for Seamus. Seamus and Mary Ann came to the door together, they were dressed for church.

"Some catchers just left my shop!"

"We saw them pass by" said Seamus, "I've sent young Tommy, the tailor's son from next door to tell Pastor Hubbs at Sandwich Baptist. Mary Ann will go to church alone today in the carriage, I'm getting my horse now and will join you."

"Good", said Scott, "Poppa's telling the Sheriff. I figure we can all meet at Peter's farm."

After a hot meal, a bath, warm dry clothes, and a good night's sleep, the three men seemed better in the morning. Peace didn't stay long for them. While Ruth cooked breakfast for her family and the guests, Shadow started yipping, and running around the house in a fit of excitement. Soon Ruth heard the unmistakable sound of hound dogs baying, horses neighing, hooves clomping and of strange men yelling.

Daniel grabbed Shadow, and held him quiet and close to him. "Daniel, take Sammy and Shadow with you in your room, stay there and keep Shadow quiet." Ruth told him.

She then went to her room and took her shotgun from its hiding place. When this project of helping the refugee people had started getting busier three years ago, Peter took her and Sarah aside and taught them each how to shoot straight and how to take care of their very own guns, the new shotguns. He held many practice sessions over the last few years to keep their skills sharp. Occasionally, the women needed their new skill. This was the first time Ruth would have to confront people alone.

Ruth opened the curtains a slit at the kitchen door facing the barn to get just a hint of what was going on. She didn't see any local men, so she knew Jackson was still on watch and would have seen the men coming, and be gone for help by now. Gordon would have taken the refugees through the secret door into the barn and up to the hiding spot in the hay loft.

The men she saw were strangers, white men, two jumped off their horses, one ran charging up to the bunkhouse door, and the other heading for the barn door, while the hound dogs were sniffing the ground. The first man started kicking at the bunkhouse door.

Ruth stormed out of her back door, stood on the stoop, cocked the leaver of her shotgun, aimed at the ground, and pulled the trigger. BOOM!! The explosion of pellets caused dirt and stones to fly all over the yard.

The men's horses and dogs jumped clear of flying pellets and debris; neighing and yelping as they jumped out of the way. The loosed horses had to be caught by the men who stayed on their mounts, and the men by the bunkhouse, and barn doors stopped, stunned.

"Get off my land!" she said, "You're frightening my children."

"Wha you doin' you crazy lady?" "Scarin' our animals like dat!" "Where're you hidin' our lazy prop'ty?" Three of the burley men spit the words back at her.

"Nobody's here, our harvest is over." She shouted back at him. "Get off my land; next time I won't aim at the ground!"

Just then, a wide eyed twelve year old Daniel appeared at the door behind her carrying a whimpering, five year old Sammy.

Cows and horses sounded from the barn, chickens clucked from the hen house. Frightened birds from the surrounding woods frantically flapped their wings as they flew higher in the air, calling warnings to each other. The hunting dogs sniffed and scratched at the ground furiously; confused. Sammy continued whimpering on the porch, and Shadow, left out of all the excitement, yipped from Daniel's room.

Ruth raised her gun and aimed at the leader. "NOW!!!" No person sounds from the barn.

Finally, slowly, the 'catchers', who were on their feet, went back and mounted their horses, and they eventually all left, grumbling.

Once the men were out of sight, Ruth took a deep breath. She lowered the muzzle of the shotgun to the floor of the porch, then turned toward the house leaning lightly on the gun and slowly lifted it up to turn it around and lean against the outside wall, muzzle facing up. Taking a still whimpering Sammy from Daniel, she asked him:

"Son, please bring a few chairs out here on the porch for us, I want to sit and watch a while."

"Okay Momma, do you think they'll come back?"

"I don't know."

She decided not to say anything to him about his taking Sammy outside with him. His seemed to be a better idea.

✦

Jackson had set up his night watch down the road from Ruth's farm and saw the men heading for her farm. He ran to Peter's house. When he finally arrived, he saw Scott, Seamus and Sheriff Pollard with Peter.

He yelled as soon as he could be heard. "There are men heading for Ruth's farm!"

He was out of breath from running. They all stopped and looked towards Ruth's farm when they heard the one shotgun blast.

Quickly, the men, all on their horses, grabbed the horse they had ready for Jackson, and met him. Jackson quickly mounted the extra saddled horse as Scott handed him a long gun.

Peter called back to Sarah, "Keep watch, more men will be coming to help, send them to Ruth's farm."

"Okay, God be with you all." She answered him.

The five men, each armed with long guns, galloped down Peter's lane, at the main road they turned towards Ruth's farm. Soon they met the angry catchers riding towards them from Ruth's farm.

Scott, Seamus, Jackson, Sheriff Pollard, and Peter arranged their horses to stand side by side. They all sat back on their horses, guns trained on the approaching party and blocking the way of the intruders.

"Who are you and where are you from?" demanded Sheriff Pollard.

"We lookin' for our prop'ty that passed by this way las' night." The spokesman replied.

The Sheriff slowly shifted forward and back again on his horse and asked: "How can *property* pass by?"

"Wi'll git our prop'ty back if we have to search ev'y house in this here area." He spoke slowly with a drawl and as if he had authority. "You people have no right to keep our prop'ty from us. Looks to me like you have some of our prop'ty with you right here." He added, nodding at Jackson and Peter.

"This is NOT your country, its CANADA, and you have NO RIGHT to search private property, or to take FREE PEOPLE into slavery here; now GO HOME!"

"They not free, they our slaves, and wa're takin' our prop'ty back!" With that retort, the leader raised his gun against the local men.

Scott anticipated the leader's movement, aimed quickly and shot the gun out of the leader's hand. His hand snapped up in pain as the gun dropped to the ground, and blood spurted from his wrist.

Quickly the other men started raising their guns to fight back as the leader jumped down from his horse to retrieve his gun. Several more shots were exchanged between the two groups of men.

Jackson also jumped down from his horse and grabbed the dropped gun before the leader was able to get it. Sheriff Pollard moved closer on his horse to the leader and held his rifle against the leader's head as he stooped down and to retrieve his gun.

"Why you lettin' that *slave* git my gun?" The leader snarled the words to Sheriff Pollard.

"They's NO slav'ry here, I's a FREE man!" Jackson said forcefully, and proudly.

"We've been telling you that. You're not taking ANYONE from Canada back into slavery" said the Sheriff.

"Oh no, they's mo' coming!" one of the catchers moaned as he held his arm, which was also hit in the melee.

The 'catchers' looked up to see the local reinforcements from Sandwich First Baptist Church, and other close neighbours who heard the news and the gunshots coming from behind the local men to help. The catchers then turned around and saw more reinforcements coming from behind them from the direction of Sandwich Town. The reinforcements totalled about twenty men.

Amazed the posse included black and white men, the 'catchers' realized they were outnumbered and the locals were serious about stopping them. The results were clear as the men were relieved of their weapons. The Sheriff brought out several handcuffs and had each 'catcher' handcuffed on their horse and the horses, as well as the dogs, tied together with rope in order for the local posse to accompany them to the ferry which was located at the foot of Brock Street in town.

Sheriff Pollard recruited several other men for the errand. Even though two 'catchers' were wounded in the melee, the locals decided to just tie up the wounds take them over the border. They would be left to take care of themselves.

By the time Daniel came out with the three chairs, the sound of gunfire echoed from down the road towards the Berry's farm.

A little while later, as Ruth and her sons sat on the porch awaiting news; Peter came down the lane, his horse at a brisk trot. Ruth rose from her chair.

"It's okay now, our men are escorting them to the ferry!" he hollered, while jumping off his horse.

"I heard the gunshots, is anyone of ours hurt Peter?" Ruth asked.

As Peter ran toward the bunkhouse he answered, "No, but they have two wounded. They aren't too bad, so we told everyone to just get out of Canada West now — or they'll go to jail! All clear up there in the loft!" Peter yelled opening the bunkhouse door.

Slowly and carefully, the men hiding in the barn came down from the loft and out through the secret door to the bunkhouse. Soon they appeared with Gordon leading them from the bunkhouse door.

"We figure this should give you the time you need to rest before moving inland. The 'catchers', if they do come back will need a few days to heal and re-group." Peter added to the men.

Turning to Gordon he added: "Gordon, would you please go to my farm and tell Sarah we are okay, and to bring the children here?"

"Sure Peter! I'll tell my family too!" Gordon said as he went to the barn to get his horse and leave to spread the good news. "We'll be back with some food for the celebration!"

Relieved, Ruth went back to the kitchen to finish breakfast, which was by now a late breakfast, and church would be held at home.

Soon they were all sitting outside at her long table which she used at harvest time when she had extra help on the farm. For the first time since the new refugees came Ruth had a chance to really meet the three new men. It was a relaxing meal bathed under the late morning sunlight and a hint of a breeze.

With the sudden release of tension the three men started to smile a bit, and looked around with a sense of wonder at their newly adopted country in the daylight. The scenery must have been very different from what they knew. The leaves on the trees were starting to turn colour. Sammy made it his business to introduce Shadow to everyone there.

Later, Ruth looked out her kitchen window at the scene of her guests interacting with her children as she tidied up from the late breakfast. She had seen many faces pass through her doors the last several years. Most of the people she met were just passing through. They were brought to her for hiding, and then quickly moved inland to safer territory and she didn't really get to know them. The people, who landed here and felt safe, usually stayed with others at first. She would meet them in town, see them settle down and become a part of the community. Like Jackson, these people she would really get to know.

The new men said their names were Joe, Tom and Titus, they told of coming from two different plantations in Mississippi. The men left during the Easter celebration this year and it was now early October, they had been travelling and hiding for over five months. They also told of the different people, the 'conductors' who guided them, and the 'station masters' who helped hide them. These people would help feed and shelter them along the way.

"Da Conductors all just kep tellin' us to foller the Nort' Star 'till we get to Canada." Joe told the others around the table. "Now here we is! Under the Nort' Star!"

As the animated conversation continued around the table, Ruth remembered back in 1833, a year before emancipation. A couple, Thornton and Lucie Blackburn escaped from the South and settled in Detroit for two years. Suddenly they were re-captured, arrested and jailed in Detroit. With the cooperation of the black communities of Detroit, Amherstburg and Sandwich, they were both helped to escape from jail in Detroit and carried here.

More trouble came when Mr. Blackburn was arrested here at the behest of the Michigan Territorial Governor as he requested extradition to the Unites States. He had to sit in the Essex County jail, just down on the corner of Sandwich and Brock Street, near the ferry, while the Michigan Territorial Governor made a formal request for his return. Soon the message was sent that the Lieutenant Governor of the then, Upper Canada, Major General Sir John Colborne refused the request.

Once free, the Blackburn's quickly moved to the newly incorporated city of Toronto where they felt safer. By 1837, Mr. Blackburn became the owner operator of the first taxi cab company in Toronto. His cabs were small buggies drawn with one horse.

The most important result of this story is that a precedent was set. Even before Emancipation, the Government of Canada would not return the refugees. The next result is that the residents here started to become more organized in order to help the refugees who wanted to come to Canada.

That's not to say that all the residents here were willing to help, some were, and some were not. Some, like Martin were downright surly, he was unwilling and uncooperative.

She briefly wondered where he was, and what the letters were all about. She then decided her life was better without him. To tell the truth, she felt more comfortable not knowing. Now that he was gone, she was able to open her home whenever the need arose for the refugees.

The last five years have been busy, but a good busy. Her children were happy and growing strong and healthy. She felt she was really useful in the cause. They seemed to be getting busier here all the time!

The conversation around the outside table was getting more animated. After Gordon spread the word, Sarah, Josh, and Anna, and their new baby, Adam, only one year old came with some food from their home, accompanied by their new puppy, Chance. Jackson, Angus, and a few others joined the group. Later they expected the men who had accompanied the 'catchers' to the ferry.

Gordon returned with his wife, Patricia, and their two children along with more food! All and all, when the various families involved arrived there was a big crowd from the neighbouring community to meet these new refugees before they had to leave.

Most of the time it didn't happen this way, just stop and carry them through, today was a gift, a harvest gift of safety for the refugees, as well as the helpers!

Maybe because it was a Sunday and people heard through the various churches about the goings on at Ruth's farm, but more people gathered than anyone expected! The local church members seemed to gather after their regular services, and they came with food and beverage, and more tables and chairs! It seemed there was going to be church again at the farm in honour of Joe, Tom, and Titus!

Josh and Daniel joined with some of the other older children who arrived with their parents, and they were all quickly pressed into the duty of setting new tables and chairs for the extra people.

The various women and girls all gathered in the kitchen and at the outside pit for roasting meat for the large meal which would come later. Adding to the experience, Anna joined Sammy and they both concentrated on introducing Shadow and his brother Chance to everyone there!

When the meal preparations were under way, three of the clergymen who were present today gathered to plan a service of thanksgiving. There was much to be thankful for this morning. They were thankful for the safety of the travellers who arrived last night, the men who participated in protecting the new arrivals this morning, and the success of their mission.

The three clergymen who planned the service were: Pastor Michael Burke from Sandwich Methodist Church, Pastor John Hubbs, from Sandwich First Baptist Church, and Sheriff Richard Pollard, the Priest of St. John's Anglican Church.

Pastor Burke owns the farm closer to the town of Sandwich from Ruth's with his wife, Kathleen. Pastor Burke bought about three tracts together from the Band at the same time as Samuel Patterson bought his tracts. When one of their sons Gordon, was married, he was given the tract located between theirs and Ruth's for his own. Gordon and his wife, Patricia, have two children, Jacob, nine years old, and Jennifer, seven years old.

Pastor John Hubbs is one of the founders of Sandwich First Baptist Church. He and his wife, Helen, and their children live with her father, Mr. Henry Brown on his farm located a little downriver from the town of Sandwich. Pastor Hubbs brought the Baptist teachings from the South when he crossed the Detroit River many years ago, and his father-in-law encouraged his starting the church here.

Sherriff Richard Pollard is the Priest and an ordained Deacon of St. John's Anglican Church, as well as the part-time Sherriff of Sandwich Town.

Father Pollard began in prayer:
"Thank you Lord for the mercies you have bestowed upon we, your servants today. Thank You for the safety we enjoyed today and thank You for the safety of our new brothers, Joe, Tom, and Titus who have now found freedom here. Thank You for bringing them to us, and be with them on the next leg of their journey. Bless us your servants in this town of Sandwich and the job You have entrusted to us of helping the refugees from slavery.

"Thank You for the food that is being prepared for us today, and for those who are preparing it for the health of our bodies. Join us in this time of praise and worship for the gifts You have given us today, in Jesus name, Amen."

Many people came armed with drums, guitars, fiddles and tambourines in anticipation of the praise music. Daniel and Josh brought out their guitars, and joined many of the other young people in singing praises.

They were pressed into service when Pastor John Hubbs and Jackson led those gathered in songs of praise. The people at the farm rocked and rolled with the movement of the music:

"Go Down Moses"
Go Down Moses — 'Way down in Egypt land, tell ole Pharaoh to let my people go — When Israel was in Egypt's land, let my people go — oppressed so hard they could not stand –Let my people go — Thus spoke the Lord bold Moses said Let my people go — If not I'll smite your first born dead — Let my people go — Go down Moses, 'Way down in Egypt's land — Let my people go.

Then they moved into:
"Every Time I Feel De Spirit"

Ev'ry time I feel de spirit move in' in my heart, I will pray, O ev'ry time I feel de spirit move in' in my heart, I will pray. Upon De Mountain my Lord spoke, out o' his mouth came fire and smoke. An' all around me look so shine, Aska my Lord if all was mine — Jordan River chilly, cold, Chill a de body but not de soul. Ev'ry time I feel de spirit, move in' in my heart I will pray.

The people swayed and joyfully sang along with the leaders. When the music stopped, they prepared themselves to hear today's message.

Pastor Michael Burke from the Methodist Church gave the sermon for today.

"My dear neighbours and friends who worship Our Lord and Saviour, Jesus Christ. Welcome to this service of praise and worship on this glorious day to thank Our Lord for this day of safety, and victory for the cause of helping our new neighbours; Titus, Tom, and Joe. We welcome these newest citizens of Canada West.

"The main scripture today is taken from the Book of James. James 1:12 & 13 & 17. In this scripture James is telling us that he who has weathered the troubles of life is blessed and he will receive the Crown of Life which God has promised us. James also assures us that God does not give us these troubles.

"This day, and this impromptu service is a gift. We also welcome you, our wonderful friends and neighbours who have come here to surround us with your love and fellowship. Please share with us in our joy and our thankfulness to the Lord for today's blessing.

"As it says in the scripture today, God does not give us our troubles. He, if we have faith in Him, and trust Him, will show us the way out of our troubles. Furthermore, He will grant us the strength to endure and finally triumph over that trouble. God also gives us the strength to endure the troubles as long as it takes to overcome that trouble. This promise is from I Corinthians 10:13.

"I don't want to talk long today, but just remind us all that we were not alone protecting our new friends today. God and His angels were guiding and protecting us every step of the way. We were warned on time, got messages on time, and were able to be ready for the encounter. And all this happened with the help and guidance of Our Lord. We are only cogs in the wheel of the escape route planned for the freeing of our new friends from further suffering in their lives; and helping them to achieve the freedom they so desire.

"We thank You God for the blessings You have given us today. We thank You for the bounty of food we are about to receive right now. We also ask that You continue bless us in our continued efforts to protect and help the others who will be coming in their quest for a life of freedom.

"I will close with another grace: Thank You, Our Lord for the food from the bountiful harvest You have bestowed upon us this year, and bless it to our bodies. Please grant us a wonderful time of fellowship today, with You and each other. Grant us Lord a safe trip home from this fellowship and health and during this week ahead, until we meet again. Amen."

When Pastor Burke finished, they sang a much beloved song of praise in closing:

"When I Survey the Wondrous Cross"

"When I survey the wondrous cross, on which the Prince of glory died, my richest gain I count but loss, and pour contempt on all my pride.

"Forbid it, Lord, that I should boast, save in the death of Christ my God: all the vain things that charm me most, I sacrifice them to His blood.

"See, from His head, His hands, His feet, sorrow and love flow mingled down: did e'er such love and sorrow meet, or thorns compose so rich a crown?

"Were the whole realm of nature mine that were a present far too small: Love so amazing so divine, demands my soul, my life, my all?"

After the service, they began the serious business of serving, and then eagerly demolishing an abundance of food. The glorious pastime of renewing friendships and meeting new friends and neighbours went on as the community listened to the stories from the new arrivals. They then shared new stories from the neighbours as they also repeated old stories for the newcomers to the community.

It was not a late evening, children had to be put to bed and the farmers had to get up early for the day ahead. Store owners had to open their businesses, and older children had to attend school in the morning.

Extra tables and chairs were put away, and borrowed ones, packed up to be returned. The leftover food was divided out for each home. Ruth and her boys were exhausted and it didn't take much for everyone to settle down to bed. Even Shadow didn't need any encouragement to crawl into bed with Sammy.

Monday morning everything was back to normal, except for the extra food Ruth had to prepare, Sarah and some of the other local ladies came by to help with the noon and evening meals.

Taima came by as usual, after Daniel came home from school to help him. When he arrived, he heard there were new people who would be moved tomorrow. Taima didn't come on Sundays anymore; he was married now, and took the day off. Daniel was now old enough to handle things by himself for one day. Things remained quiet in the community.

Early Tuesday morning, Gordon and Scott came to move Tom, Titus and Joe to the Band. They had arranged for two of the Band members to take the men to safety further inland to Chatham. Usually only one man took the trip, but they figured the task might require more security this time because of the problem on Sunday morning.

They showed the hiding place built in the wagon to the men who crawled in, and then the men all settled in for the ride. The idea of taking the men to the Band members to make the larger part of the trip, was to hopefully confuse the efforts of any people following the travellers, it also gave the refugees a rest and a chance to stretch their legs.

Ruth, and Gordon's wife Patricia, packed some food and water for the trip. The two women saw the travellers off as the wagon moved slowly down the lane away from the farm.

After the men left, Ruth and Patricia decided to have a cup of tea before Patricia had to leave for home and her own family.

"I know this leg of the trip is not as dangerous as the previous ones. I always worry when Gordon goes away on these errands. At least this is not as long a trip for him and he will be home later today." Patricia said.

"I know how you feel," answered Ruth. "You never really know what lies ahead."

"Momma," Daniel said, as he was getting ready to meet Josh for school, "Josh and me want to go down to the river after school today and catch some fish for dinner tonight. Do you mind?"

"Sure son that will be a good treat. Have fun!" Ruth answered.

"If you catch any extra Daniel, don't forget us!" called Patricia with a laugh.

"Okay Auntie Patricia we'll try!" Daniel hollered over his shoulder as he ran off to meet Josh.

When Patricia left, the two women returned to their regular chores. Ruth went on with her main job of running the house and farm. Later she was hanging up extra sheets from the bunkhouse visitors, and Sammy was 'helping' to carry baskets of laundry. Shadow carried on as 'chief morale officer' by jumping around and acting like a puppy. She was in a good mood, the wind was good, not too strong, and the clothes would blow well and dry quickly.

The everyday work would be invigorating because of the natural relief the whole community felt after the danger of the encounter with the 'catchers', and the good result.

Now the three men were safely on their way to their new life. She happily continued her jobs with her support staff of Sammy and Shadow, who 'helped' with the milking, and feeding of the animals as well as cleaning the barn and house.

After school was out, and the work with Taima was completed, Daniel and Josh picked up their poles at Josh's house and headed for their favorite fishing spot. The cove on the Berry's land; the best fishing within walking distance was still deep in Berry's Cove.

Taima said he couldn't join them today but he would another time. The best time to fish was early in the morning, and they liked to go then during the summer. Now that school was back this was the best time for the boys.

A few years ago, the local men who helped in the abolitionist's project were trying to find a way to better shield the cove from the main river.

Unfortunately, so far no one had any good answers.

Occasionally, the residents along the river would see some row boats. They carried white people who appeared to be fishing and move close to the shore. They would go back and forth along the shore for a while, and then move away, back toward the Detroit shore.

Fortunately, God still seemed to take the shielding of the cove into His hands, and — so far — no wrong person from Detroit seemed to find it. The cove was also protected from common view on the Canadian shore, by virtue of being on the Berry's land and well away from the main road. Berry's Cove was still a safe place to land for refugees from the South.

"My Poppa says maybe the United States will stop the slavery in my lifetime, and then we won't have to fight those 'catchers' anymore." Josh said. "I was worried when we heard those gun shots from your house and again from the road on Sunday morning. I didn't know if you and your Momma and Sammy were safe."

"We were worried too. All those men came with their big hunting dogs, looking for the refugees, and yelling at my Momma. Later, when the gunshots came from the road, we didn't know where they were coming from and who would be coming back." Daniel continued. "Now you and I are getting older, and stronger, I hope your Poppa lets us do more to help out too. It would be good if we just didn't have to hide

33

people anymore. People could just come and go as they please like you and me."

"Yea, that's the best thing." Josh agreed.

The boys settled down at their favorite spot in the cove. There was a little grassy rise under the shade of an old maple tree at the end of the shore, where they could sit on the ground with their polls hanging over the water's edge and their feet a little lower down the shore, almost like a chair.

Being that it was getting to be late fall, the leaves were falling off the tree, and since it was not all that sunny today, they didn't need shade anyway. They sat there for a couple of hours, the leaves that had already fallen from the tree, formed a cushion on the ground.

The boys were sometimes talking, sometimes laughing with excitement over a good fish, and mostly just quiet and thoughtful.

Eventually, the boys caught enough fish for the two families, and even enough for Mr. and Mrs. Burke and their children for tonight's evening meal and slowly went on their way. First they went to see Mrs. Burke and give her some fish, where Jacob made them promise to bring him with them next time.

"He's too little to come with us, he's only nine." Daniel complained, as they walked down the lane from the Burke house.

"I know," said Josh, "but he doesn't have a big brother like us!"

"Your right." answered Daniel slowly. "Your Poppa, and Taima took us when we were little, I guess we should be good big brothers for him and take him sometimes."

The next stop was to Josh's house so Daniel could drop off his pole, and then Daniel went home with his fish, alone. There would be plenty of fresh fish for the evening meal at three homes tonight!

November 1843
CHAPTER 3

Soon, it was November, the air was getting colder, and the first freeze had happened, snow was in the air. During the second week of the month, late afternoon on Tuesday two strangers came to town.

One was older than the other, dark, but greying hair, wrinkles starting on his face. The younger man had light brown hair, and he was slight of build. Both were dressed for comfortable travel; casual pants, shirt, and heavy jacket for the cooler weather. After arriving, the men rode up and down the length of Sandwich Street about three times, trying to get their bearings.

They stopped in at the Post Office and talked to the Postmaster for a while. They then decided to find a room to rent on Sandwich Street. They chose the Public House which served food, and had rooms to rent upstairs. They made arrangements to stay for three days.

Early the next morning, Wednesday, they stopped at Seamus and Mary Ann's store.

"We're looking for Martin Logan, where does he live?" The older man said.

"Martin, he left town about five years ago." Mary Ann replied.

"He's married, where is his wife?"

"At the end of town the farms start, it's about four or five tracts down, there is a sign: 'Logan Farm'."

As soon as the men left her store, Mary Ann rushed to the storeroom in the back and called to Seamus. "I'm afraid there might be trouble for Ruth. Two men came in the store and were asking about Martin and wanted to know where Ruth lived. I told them, but I'm thinking maybe Martin has found some trouble somewhere. I don't like the looks of them."

"You mind the store, and I'll go and tell Sheriff Pollard and then Peter and Sarah, they're closer to Ruth than anyone."

"Well that came sooner than I expected." The Sheriff told Seamus, "A few weeks ago, just before the 'catchers' came Samuel told me Ruth was getting letters for Martin. He said she just returned them. Ruth didn't want to know where he was or what he was doing."

"Do you want me to go with you?" Seamus said, "I was thinking of telling Peter and Sarah, since they are closer to Ruth than anyone else around here."

"I think I'll go myself, at first — oh — I'll have to think of a reason for being there as I go — uh — let me feel out the situation while I'm there. — No — better yet, you're right, why don't we ride out there together. You go on to Peter's; I'll meet you there after I see what's going on at Ruth's farm."

✦

"Momma, we have visitors!" Sammy called. Ruth and Sammy were feeding the chickens in the coup beside the barn.

The two strangers arrived in her laneway on horseback. Ruth stopped what she was doing and studied the two men as they rode slowly towards the barn which shared a wall with the coup. Both men had a serious 'air' about them. They were dressed again in casual travel clothes. She didn't recognize them at all. Bringing Sammy along with her, she closed the gate to the coup and moved slowly to meet the men.

Quietly, she said to Sammy: "Stay near me son." Ruth watched with apprehension as they moved down the lane towards her and Sammy.

The two men rode their horses slowly down the lane and further onto Ruth's property.

"Are you Ruth Logan?" the older man asked.

Sammy ran to catch Shadow who was running up to the two strangers. When Sammy caught Shadow he clumsily picked him up and then turned to join his mother.

"Yes. Who are you?" Ruth said her arm resting on Sammy's shoulder.

"We have some business with your husband, Martin Logan. I sent some letters, but they were returned with no answer." He replied. "Who's your little friend here? What's your puppy's name boy?"

"Shadow," Sammy said hesitantly, now leaning against Ruth's skirt. He was precariously holding the fast growing and squiggly puppy under his front legs with both arms.

"You addressed the letters to Martin, I never read his mail, and he didn't leave a forwarding address." Ruth answered as she held Sammy closer.

"He left here five years ago, and didn't say where he was going. He just said he was never coming back. Martin has never had any contact with me since then. You still haven't said who you are, or what your business is."

"Shadow's a good name boy! How old is he?" The younger man was talking again. He dismounted from his horse, and walked toward the puppy and Sammy, then crouched down to Sammy's level.

Ruth clutched Sammy closer pulling him further away from the man. "Leave my son alone. Tell me who are you and state your business here." Ruth was getting more nervous.

"I need to find Martin. He didn't give you any idea where he was heading? We thought Martin would contact us before now. Did he leave a package or papers behind?"

The older man was talking again. The younger man ignored Ruth while petting Shadow, who was always willing to accept more attention.

"Martin took everything he had of value, he only left some clothes, and I cleared all his things out years ago. Get away from my son!" Ruth told the younger man louder.

Just then, out of the corner of her eye, behind the men, Ruth spotted Sheriff Pollard coming down the lane, his horse at a slow walk. She relaxed, help was near. When he got closer to them the Sheriff called: "Hi Ruth! Who are your visitors? I just came down to talk about a planning meeting in town later this week."

"Hi Sheriff, these men say they have business with Martin, but they won't tell me who they are or anything about their business. I want this younger one to get away from Sammy and Shadow."

The men looked at each other and seemed concerned when Ruth identified Sheriff Pollard to them, but the younger of the two stood up and recovered quickly.

"Hi Sheriff, I'm John Daily." He said as he offered his hand to the Sheriff. "And this is my boss, David Johnson. We're from east in London, Middlesex County. We were carrying out some business dealings with

Martin Logan. We expected to hear from him at least three years ago concerning our plans. We thought he was still living here."

The Sheriff dismounted his horse and shook hands with John Daily. "No one has heard or seen him around here for five years." The Sheriff said. "Mrs. Logan has been running the farm and raising her sons by herself all this time."

The newly identified David said. "We were really hoping she might have some information about where he would have gone." Turning towards Ruth he said. "What direction did he take from here? Did he talk about any other city or town where he might go?"

"Frankly David, he was very closed-mouthed about any plans he had, and didn't give any hints about where to look for him." Ruth said. "We argued the night he left, and I didn't look out the window to see which direction he went."

"I was hoping you might have more information than that." David said a little disappointed. "Did he leave any papers or a package behind?"

"No, he left nothing behind at all." Ruth replied.

"It looks like Mrs. Logan has no information for you here." Sheriff Pollard picked up Sammy who was still holding Shadow; which left quite a squirmy armful to handle. "Maybe it's time you left town. I always thought he might have gone west. You never seem to hear from people when they go west, and Martin seemed to want to be gone forever."

"I was wondering if there's a place to rent a room around here." John said. "Or maybe you can rent us a room in your bunkhouse there."

"I'm a woman living alone, and will not let strangers stay in my bunkhouse." Ruth said. "The only people I let stay there are people I know, and that's only at harvest time."

"If that's what you say." John grinned as he mounted his horse.

The two men turned to leave, mumbling to each other on their way down the lane.

"I don't like it." The Sheriff said. "They gave you no information, and could have given you false names. They also seem to think he left information behind. Did he leave any papers or packages?"

"No Richard, I cleaned our room out the morning after he left. There's been so many changes made on the house, barn and bunkhouse, someone would have discovered any packages or valuables he left hidden before now.

"I'm worried Martin might have said something about my thoughts on the refugees. I didn't hide people in the bunkhouse until after he left, but I didn't like the way the younger man said 'If that's what you say'. I wonder if they have an information source from here."

"I noticed that too." The Sheriff said. "I'm going down to Peter's house. Seamus and I rode out here together and Seamus said he heard the men have already rented a room in town. I think they were just trying to get information. Seamus is at Peter's waiting to see me now. I take it Daniel's in school today?"

"Yes." Said Ruth.

"I'll send someone here to keep an eye on you tonight and until those men leave town. They were too interested in Sammy. I'm going to take him down to Peter's for now until I can get you more help. Maybe you should pick Daniel up from school today, and then stay at Peter and Sarah's house until we get things in place for you here." The Sheriff replied.

"Okay," She said. "How would you like to play with Anna and Adam today, Sammy? Let me take Shadow and we'll meet you at Anna's house with Daniel later." She said as she took Shadow from Sammy's arms. "I'll just finish with the work here, and leave to get Daniel."

Ruth actually had a different idea. When she finished her work, she packed some clothes for her and the boys. She then piled Shadow in her wagon, and headed for the school to pick Daniel up early.

"But Momma, we're having a rehearsal for the Christmas play this afternoon, and Josh and I have to practice our song!" Daniel complained.

"I know son, but Josh will have to rehearse without you this time. Something happened today, I'll tell you about it when we start on our way."

When Ruth, Daniel, and Shadow arrived at Peter and Sarah's house, her plan was to pick up Sammy and head directly for Amherstburg.

"Come on Sammy, we have to go to Uncle Samuel, and Auntie Elizabeth's."

"No!" Sammy complained. "Anna and I are helping Auntie Sarah!"

"We have to go to Uncle Samuel and Auntie Elizabeth's right now!" Ruth countered. To Sarah she said: "I have to go to my aunt and uncle's until those men have left town. Those two men frightened me. I have to make sure my children are safe. I'll come back myself tomorrow to tend to animals here."

Sarah sat Ruth down on a chair in their drawing room. She calmly told Ruth that she and Peter had discussed another plan with Seamus and the Sheriff.

"Sheriff Pollard wants you to wait here. Peter has left to ask the people at the Band to look out for trouble and then head for Amherstburg to prepare your uncle and aunt for your arrival. He will also let them know about the two visitors.

"The Sheriff will have some men posted at your house by tonight. He wants you to stay here, and is arranging for two men to accompany you to Amherstburg early tomorrow morning. No one wants you to try that trip alone right now. The Sheriff is also checking in to where the men are staying. He wants to make sure they are occupied elsewhere, so they cannot follow you to your uncle's house." Sarah said.

Ruth had to admit their plan was safer than her frantic plan.

Peter returned late that night and told Ruth and Sarah everything was ready in Amherstburg, and the People of the Band would be keeping an eye on anyone who passed by their land. Earlier, the Sheriff sent a messenger to tell them he had arranged for some local men to watch her farm until her return. He had also arranged for Scott and Jackson to accompany her and her sons to Amherstburg the next morning.

Everyone in the Berry household was up by daybreak the following morning. Anna and Sammy did not really understand the threat to the Logan's, and Josh and Daniel's understanding was not much better.

"Do we really have to go to Uncle Samuel's house?" Daniel complained. "How long will we stay? I don't want to miss out on being in the Christmas Concert this year. Josh and I are shepherds and we get to sing together."

"Yes!" Josh added, "Daniel can stay here with us like he did when we fixed up your house! I really don't want to sing the song alone! Daniel and I are best friends, we can watch out for each other!"

"Oh my dear hearts, I know how much you boys will miss each other, but we adults are still trying to find out what these strangers are planning. We do know they are interested in Daniel and Sammy and right now, my sons have to be hidden from them."

Ruth was crushed. She and Sarah exchanged quick glances. They knew how close the two boys have grown over the years and had discussed how they thought their sons' friendship would probably be a lifetime one. What a gift, to have a friendship that endured from early childhood and last a lifetime.

Scott and Jackson arrived in good time. Quickly, Ruth's family all climbed in her wagon. They used Ruth's horses to drive the wagon, and the men brought their own horses because they planned to return to

Sandwich Town as soon as possible. Scott drove, and Daniel rode Scott's horse. Jackson tied his horse to the back of the wagon and rode inside to keep an eye on Sammy and Shadow.

The Berry family stood in the yard and watched the wagon ride down the lane. Peter wrapped one arm around Anna's shoulder and the other around Sarah's as she held Adam. Josh grabbed Chance who tried to follow Shadow, and held him close as he stood on his own and watched his friend and Chance watched his brother leave. Daniel turned back several times as he tearfully rode Scott's horse alongside the wagon.

In the bed of the wagon, as they settled in for the long ride, Jackson covered himself and Sammy in an old handmade quilt Ruth kept there for the winter months. Once they were both settled, he pulled out his wood and knife to start his true love, whittling. Sammy watched, transfixed while Jackson busied himself and made some little wood animal figures during the long ride. Shadow settled down from his initial excitement, and finally just lay down beside Sammy while he watched Jackson, and enjoyed the different routine.

When the party passed by the Band property, there was plenty of activity. They knew there were many more watchers than could be seen from the road. The travellers waved at the watchers some of whom were on horseback and huddled in robes against the bitter cold, the watchers waved back. The People of the Band were keeping an eye out for any unusual travellers on the road.

It started snowing shortly after they passed the Band property. By the time they arrived at the Patterson farm just west of Amherstburg the snow was starting to pile up, as the first snows usually are, with big, wet heavy flakes. It was hard for the narrow wheels of the wagon to hold a straight line in the messy dump of snow. As they drove up the lane towards Uncle Samuel and Aunt Elizabeth's house everyone was ready for a good hot meal.

From the lane leading to the big farm house they could see the surrounding roofed veranda holding several chairs and tables for summer sitting. The furniture was covered for the winter months now. The veranda wound around the back where they would be able to leave the wagon in the barn and take care of the horses. The men and Daniel stayed to unhitch the wagon and prepare to feed and bed the horses while Ruth and Sammy rushed through the snow to the kitchen door. Uncle Samuel hugged Ruth and Sammy quickly, as he passed them on the way to meet the men in the barn.

In the house, Ruth and Sammy were greeted by Aunt Elizabeth and the family cook, Freda.

"There you are!" Aunt Elizabeth exclaimed. "Finally, we've been worried about you travelling in this."

"Look at this! Jackson made this fox for me and is going to show me how to make things too while we travel!" Sammy shouted to Aunt Elizabeth and Freda. He was very impressed with Jackson's talent, and was looking forward to his own lessons.

When things were settled in the barn, Jackson exited last. He stopped and marvelled at the untouched snow covering the fields. The sun had come out and its rays bounced off the blanket of snow leaving a sea of shimmering stars. He leaned on a nearby fence rail drinking in the sight as he thought: "They toll me to foller the Nort Star, so dis is what it's like under the Nort Star."

"Come on Jackson! Lunch is ready!" Scott called. Jackson left his reverie and turned to follow Scott.

Later, at the table, Sammy continued his chant about the carving and passed his new prize around for all to see.

Daniel, who had been watching the whittling from horseback while they travelled, took the little fox from Sammy and admired it too. "Oh Jackson, I like it, can I have lessons too?"

Uncle Samuel took it next and studied the small carving. "Jackson, that's good work, are you putting some of your work at the general store to sell?" He said.

"I dint tink of it. I been whittlin' these li'l things, since I's a boy and I jus' been givin' dem away." Jackson answered.

"I think you have a good business idea here." Uncle Samuel said. Turning his attention to Ruth, and Scott, he added: "Peter told me what went on yesterday, and I have hired an investigator to check up on John Daily and David Johnson, your strangers visiting from London. Maybe my investigator can figure out what they have to do with Martin, and what the big mystery is about. After the meal we can talk in my study."

Later, Jackson and Scott met Samuel in the study. Scott told Uncle Samuel.

"We left this morning when the men were still in their room. The Sheriff said they had arranged for breakfast downstairs at the Public House in town at 9:00 this morning. We decided to leave from Peter's house at daybreak. The Sheriff didn't know their plans for today." Scott volunteered. "We wanted to travel while we knew where the men were. Ruth and the Sheriff told me the younger man, John Daily was very interested in Sammy, and I think it's a good idea to keep those men away from the boys."

"I agree Scott." Uncle Samuel replied. "My investigator will be leaving first thing tomorrow morning, so I probably won't hear anything for a week or two."

"The Sheriff said they only arranged to stay for three days, but they could change that if they wanted. I just wish we could find out what they were planning with Martin." Scott added.

Later, Jackson noticed the snow had stopped, and when the sun came out its warmth started to melt the snow a bit. Scott and Jackson decided to leave for home while the weather was calm and it was still light outside.

When Scott and Jackson passed the Band territory on their way home, there was a different group of men, outwardly guarding the road.

"Did any strangers pass by today?" Scott asked his friend, Kajika. Lately, Kajika has been joining his brother, Taima who has been coming regularly to Ruth's farm to help with the horses since Martin left.

"Not yet, Scott, Peter asked us to look for two men, and older one and a younger one in his thirties. We've been watching in shifts, it's a good thing the snow's seems to be over for now! Who's your friend?"

"Oh, I didn't know you didn't know each other. Jackson, this is Kajika. This is Jackson's first Canadian winter! Kajika is a resident of the local Band. As well as being good neighbours; they help us move refugees further inland to safety when they can."

"Hi dere Kajika." Said Jackson. "Dis be ma fust snow! It be real purdy, but I dint know how cold it wus gunna be!"

The three men shared a good laugh.

"Thanks for helping us Kajika:" Scott added. "Those two men have been 'nosing' around Ruth's place asking about Martin. Martin was so against the movement, we've been worried they might be trying to find out if Ruth is involved, and how we hide and move the refugees. Stay warm and dry!"

"You also Scott, we'll be keeping watch for the men and any trouble. My brother didn't go to the farm today. Peter said there would be people watching the farm and see to the animals until Ruth returned home." Kajika answered.

Scott and Jackson went on their way, farther along the road to home Scott asked Jackson about his carvings.

"An ol' mans from the plantation start a-teachin' me how to do da whittlin' when I's jus a boy." Jackson said. "Wheneva we had a chans, he would show me how to do 'em, and later, when Ol' Leroy passed, I just kep it up. The carving ra'laxs me, and I like dat others fine pleasure from ma work."

"Do you know that Peter Berry is a carpenter?" Scott answered. "He's made most of the furniture in his house, and he and Gordon Burke have been building all the special wagons we use to transport refugees out of this area. I bet the three of you could work together and start some kind of business.

"Peter, Gordon, Ruth and most of the others around here have plenty of trees that need cutting for farming. That gives you at least three lots of wood to work with! My Poppa always says that if you can find a living doing something you love, then no matter how much or little money you make at it, you are a rich man."

"I din know Peter and Gordon were ca'penters. I jus know dem from aw wuk with da ref-aw-gees, an I tought dey was jest farmas, cins dey haf the lan." Jackson paused a bit before he added: "I'll talk to dem 'bout da carpentry, I'd also like ta try makin' bigger carvings; us'lly I jus use lil' odds and ends of wood dat I fin 'round da place. Mista Patterson had an idea 'bout sellin' ma work in da Gen'al Sto."

A few miles before they arrived at Ruth's farmhouse, darkness was starting to fall and Jackson and Scott decided to go by Ruth's house and barn, just to check things out. "I hab a bad feelin' dose men would try ta look for the thin's they tink Ruth's man left ba-hind or maybe ev'n try to wait for whoever comes to da farm."

"I agree Jackson, I'm glad we carried our weapons with us for the trip today."

When they arrived at Ruth's farm, they found Sheriff Pollard had posted four local men to guard the property; Seamus Murphy Jr., Tim Burke, Gordon's younger brother, and two sons of Pastor Hubbs, Hank and Abe Hubbs.

"The strangers did visit again." Answered Tim Burke. "They showed up around mid — morning, but were surprised to find us here to care for Ruth's animals and guard her property. It has been quiet here since then."

Hank Hubbs, Pastor John's son added: "They said they were relatives of Martin, and were worried they had not heard from him in a while. The thing is the men were more interested in searching the property than wondering where Martin was, or where Ruth and her boys had gone. Not only that, they were suspicious of some of us," With a few hand gestures highlighting his face and ending with a bow and a grin he added: "I guess some of us are just a little too dark for their liking."

Slowly shaking his head, Scott asked: "Did they get to look around at all?"

"Not on your life! We didn't let them get past the front of the yard!" Hank's brother Abe exclaimed. "We told them no one got in anywhere

here without Ruth's permission and shuffled them off the property — they were angry. I don't think we're done with them yet."

"Well," Said Scott. "At least they told you they were Martin's relatives, that's more than they said to anyone else. The only thing is we know is, they plan to stay at least another day. I wonder what else they have planned."

"We'll be ready for whatever happens." Added Seamus Jr.

"I know Ruth and her family appreciate it men." Scott said.

Jackson said: "I wus goin' to hep keep watch for Ruth, let me know if you boys need ma hep."

"Sure thing Jackson thanks for the offer." Abe Hubbs said.

"Can you come back tomorrow morning to relieve me Jackson?" Seamus Jr. asked. "I should be at my parents' store to help there tomorrow; they have some deliveries coming in."

"Sure ting Shey-mus, glad to hep." Jackson answered.

The next morning, Apenimon arrived at Peter and Sarah's front door.

"I'm carrying a message from my father. Yesterday afternoon we followed the two men you described into Amherstburg. They rode up and down the street, stopping at shops, and asking questions. They got a room in town, and stayed there last night.

"We are still keeping an eye out for them now, but my father wanted you to know what we have found so far, he has also sent a messenger to Samuel Patterson."

Three days later, Apenimon returned to report:

"The men spent yesterday and the day before visiting shops and talking to people around in Amherstburg, they were asking about Samuel Patterson and his family, wanted to know where he lived. Then they went to their room for a while, ate at the restaurant next to their rooming house and left town in the direction of London.

"They didn't try to go to the Patterson home at all. Samuel has people guarding his home and property."

A little over two weeks later, it was just three weeks before Christmas and Samuel's expressions went from a frown to amazement to horror as he studied the papers from London. His investigator, Bradley Cummings, and his lawyer, Thomas Manning sat with him in his study.

Elizabeth was wondering what resulted from the trip to London as she and Freda worked in the kitchen on a noon meal for everyone. Ruth and her boys left last week, when the Sheriff and Peter were sure the two men would stay away for a while.

"Oh my Lord in heaven, I didn't expect this. What about Ruth's marriage? Is she really a married women, and what about Daniel and Sammy?" Samuel was confounded. "Are there any other wives he collected? What about his wife in London? How has she been getting along? Does she have children with him?"

Bradley Cummings, the investigator answered.

"The younger man who travelled down here, John Daley is the brother of Anna-Lynn Logan. Martin married her first. There are three children, Shannon, 16, Gabriel, 12, and Jeanne, 9. Since Ruth's marriage happened after the first one Martin was obviously trying to balance two families at the same time.

Right now, we aren't sure whether or not Anna-Lynn was aware of Ruth all along. Since John Daley was down here with David Johnson, we can assume she knows about Ruth and her family by now. We haven't learned of any other marriages."

Thomas Manning, the lawyer continued.

"Legally, Ruth has never been married, so that answers your old questions about leaving all your property to Ruth. The boys can keep their name of Logan, since Martin is their father, but they can also legally change their names to Patterson.

"Now we know the truth, Martin has no rights to any property of Ruth's, but as long as the boys are minors he is still able to assert his parental rights to take charge of their property."

The two men had left the hard information for the end of the meeting. Bradley continued.

"The sticky problem is with David Johnson, the man John Daley referred to as 'his boss'. David publishes a newspaper in London which promotes a pro-slavery attitude. He is known to have contacts in Detroit and in other, larger cities in the United States. He has also made it known he wants to enlarge his holdings into Essex County to be closer to the United States.

"Martin may have been sent down here by David to try to acquire some of your land, and use his marriage to Ruth as a means to that end. As well he could gather information on our activities to help the refugees. This could sabotage our efforts and achieve his ultimate goal of stopping the influx of refugees."

"Martin must never have planned to stay with Ruth." Samuel sighed. "I knew he wanted to control some of my property, that's why I wouldn't sign over any property or any investments for him to run. Oh my Lord, how do we tell her this?"

At the noon meal, Samuel, Mr. Manning, and Mr. Cummings broke the news to Elizabeth. She sat in her place at the table, and stared wide-eyed at the men all through the telling of the story. She then stood up and said quietly,

"To be so completely betrayed, my poor Ruth." She then ran from the table in tears.

Samuel let her go; the men then continued the conversation they had started earlier in his study.

"It is clear David and John expected information from Martin, and intend to continue Martin's goal of trying to sabotage the work we are doing here," Samuel opened, "and this is only just starting up again from where Martin left off. I'm afraid John will try to tell the boys they have siblings and try to pull them over to their side in that way."

"You'll have to be prepared for anything and everything they might throw at you Samuel." Bradley Cummings agreed, and then continued. "Are you sure Ruth's safe where she is? They might try to take the boys, Daniel is getting bigger, but Sammy is small and they are both still very young."

The two men left after the meal telling Samuel to contact either of them whenever he needed. Mr. Manning told Samuel he would prepare the new will discussed today and it would be ready to sign next week in his office. After they left, Samuel went upstairs to the bedroom he and Elizabeth shared and they comforted each other and prepared themselves for the ordeal of telling Ruth the news.

✦

It was not until the next morning a Tuesday, that Samuel and Elizabeth felt they had a good enough grip on the whole story, and their emotions to travel to Ruth's farm and tell her the result of the investigation. They made their way in the cold and blowing snow that day, the gloomy weather seemed to be appropriate for the dreadful news they had to deliver.

They stopped at the Chippewa Band Settlement, because Samuel wanted to tell Siwili first. The Band people would be instrumental in helping with this new problem. While he was at the Band, Samuel made arrangements with Siwili to bring Apenimon and Taima and meet with him and Peter in the bunkhouse at Ruth's farm this afternoon.

They then stopped at Peter's farm to invite him and Sarah to Ruth's house. He and Elizabeth had decided to tell all of them together. Elizabeth and Sarah's presence would help Ruth when she heard this devastating news.

Elizabeth and Sarah could also help Ruth while the men's separate meeting was going on in the bunkhouse. More importantly, it was time for the main characters from the original meeting west of Amherstburg a little over five years ago to meet again.

Ruth was surprised to see Samuel, Elizabeth, Peter, Sarah, Anna, and Adam all at her front door, and braving the blowing snowy weather.

"What a day to be travelling!" she exclaimed when she opened the door.

Daniel and Josh were at school, and Anna and Sammy were told by Uncle Samuel to stay busy in the living room. They were to keep an eye on Adam, who fell asleep as soon as he was settled on a quilt on the floor. Uncle Samuel was calm but very serious with the children, and they immediately realized this was an important adult meeting not to be interrupted.

"Your uncle has heard from his investigators Ruth." Aunt Elizabeth told her, as she gathered the two younger women and they all headed for the kitchen.

"We all need to sit around your kitchen table so Uncle Samuel can explain everything to you. I will start the water for tea; you and Sarah gather cups for everyone."

Ruth and Sarah followed Aunt Elizabeth to the kitchen, and obeyed her direction. Both women were struck by Aunt Elizabeth's solemn demeanour. The three women set the table for the meeting. When everything was ready Uncle Samuel and Peter sat on one side of the table, and the three women on the other side. Aunt Elizabeth made sure Ruth was seated between her and Sarah.

Uncle Samuel started talking and soon Ruth's mind went numb as she tried to process the words her Uncle was saying. He tried to fully explain the whole story.

Ruth's mind swam with the information. "Martin had a wife and child before he even met me! He was actually going home to another family all those times he left! He has three other children besides my two sons!" The fog swirling in her mind continued to flow.

"He was only trying to get at Uncle Samuel's property and money, that's why he was so mad about the farm not being ours — he wanted it to really be his! He was planning to try to stop the refugees from coming here altogether!" Ruth felt Sarah and Elizabeth's hands holding hers. Steadying her, and comforting her as she heard the nightmare unfold.

The comforting arms of those dear loved ones held her steady as she tried to process the rest.

"I was never really married at all! Sammy is still very young and never met his father, but how will Daniel take this news?" The fog swirling in her mind continued to flow.

"If his family doesn't know where he is then where is Martin now? Does his other wife know about me? What are his family's plans? Are they going to keep looking for Martin here, or will they look elsewhere?" She became dully aware of a conversation starting among the other people at the table. The fog swirling in her mind continued to flow.

"Thank you God for holding me tightly in your hands. Thank you God for giving me my dear friend Sarah and wonderful Auntie Elizabeth for loving support in this terrible time." The fog swirling in her mind continued to flow.

The two men were now getting up from the table. An echo of words from her Uncle's voice swirled into the fog.

"I see Siwili, Apenimon and Taima have just arrived, I asked them here to meet with us. Peter, we have to talk about protecting Ruth and the boys and your family and Berry's Cove." The fog swirling in her mind started to clear.

"You think — we're in danger?" Ruth said dully looking up to her uncle. She was becoming aware, but not fully engaged in the surrounding conversation.

"I don't know dear, I just want to be careful." Uncle Samuel said kindly, as he leaned across the table to pat her hand. "We want to be ready in case the London people come back and try to start trouble. We'll just be in the bunkhouse for our meeting dear. Maybe you ladies can fix us a small meal."

Wordlessly, the men moved around the large bunkhouse room. Peter and Apenimon started a fire in the wood stove for warmth. Siwili and Taima arranged chairs in the room to surround the long table which stood to one side. A row of eight bunks lined the length on the other side of the room.

Samuel gathered some cutlery, cups and dishes from the cupboard which stood near the table. Eventually, as each man finished his task, they all sat around the table.

Peter started the discussion "Just how many people know about that day, and who are they?"

"Except for my people, who were there, I have spoken to no one. My people know better than to talk openly about it." Siwili said.

"Not me." "Not me." Taima and Apenimon agreed.

"Same here" Samuel said. "I haven't even told my lawyer or my private investigator. Be careful what you say until the women come in with our meal."

Peter started. "We have to find a way to not only to protect Ruth and her boys, but to protect everyone here who is working on this project. The threat is for this whole area, not only here in Sandwich Town and Amherstburg, but everyone who is involved in the whole of Essex and Kent Counties."

"You are right Peter," Siwili agreed. "Samuel, your investigator said their intention is to prevent the work we have been doing here altogether. I would like to add to that they would also like to see me and my people disappear."

The men nodded, they knew Siwili was speaking the truth. There was quiet for some time while they all digested this news and the consequences of this information.

There was a knocking at the door and the men all turned to face it. Peter, who was closest, rose to answer it. They watched as he opened to find Sarah and Ruth carrying trays holding their noon meal.

"The food smells wonderful ladies, thank you for bringing it to us." Peter said graciously, as he and Taima, who also rose, helped them in with the heavy trays. Sarah and Ruth helped unload the trays quietly, then left the trays on the cupboard, and quickly left the men to their discussion.

"I'm thinking they won't come down here from London again until the weather breaks this spring." Samuel said, hopefully.

"I wouldn't want to count on that." Peter said. "We might have a thaw or a temporary break in the weather."

"I know you're right, Peter." Samuel sadly agreed. "We have to be especially vigilant concerning the work with the refugees, and when new people arrive, to encourage them to move further north, away from the border."

"I'm thinking we should tell the people closest to the cause. The Sheriff, Pastor Hubbs, Seamus, Gordon, and Scott what we know about the two men from London, Martin's other family, and his involvement with the publisher, David Johnson." Peter said.

"That information should be enough for them to want to help keep watch; especially when they know about Martin's involvement with David Johnson and his desire to stop the flow of refugees." Peter continued: "As far as our actions that night, we can just continue as we have been, with Apenimon and Sarah and me stating we saw him leaving town.

"Everyone living in Town at the time knows he was unhappy here. Ruth and Daniel have been saying for years he was angry, and wasn't planning to return. They also confirm that he didn't say where he was going when he left. Sarah, Ruth and Daniel only know what they saw and heard that night."

"I agree Peter." Said Samuel.

"What about Ruth, do you not think she should be told at some point this man has died?" Apenimon asked. "She is a young woman, maybe she would like to marry again someday. All these years, ever since I found his body I've felt so bad for her because she doesn't know about him."

"Things have not changed at all since that day, and with the appearance of these people from London, it can only be worse." Samuel answered. "Not any of the people from London, and several people from around here would believe his horse stumbled and he fell and hit his head on a fallen dead tree. They would much rather believe a Chippewa or Negro person killed him. The fact it happened on Chippewa land only makes it worse."

"I'm thankful the old Negro cemetery was nearby your land Siwili. I don't think he would be happy knowing where he is, but at least no one will look for him there." Peter reflected.

"Did anyone look in his saddlebags, or his bedroll?" Taima asked. "Peter, you said the men from London asked if he left a package or papers behind. Maybe he had something of importance in them."

Siwili answered him. "No, we didn't look inside. We just packed everything together. The saddlebags and bedroll are buried with him. I remember they were full, but I figured it was all just clothing."

"As far as I'm concerned, what was with him then can stay with him, and it would be too dangerous to go digging him up now." Samuel added. "According to my lawyer, Ruth has been free the entire time from any legal attachment to Martin. I see no need to tell her he's dead. At least now she knows she is free to remarry."

Apenimon finally and reluctantly agreed with the others to keep the full truth hidden from Ruth. Although he still wanted to open Martin's grave and see if the mysterious 'package' the people from London talked about was with him in the saddlebags when he died.

"As far as the present is concerned, my people can continue watching as we have been this winter." Siwili volunteered. "I think, Taima, that we should add a second visit each day to Ruth's farm. If you can't make it a second time one day, have one of the other men help out."

"Thank you Siwili, I agree." Added Peter. "It has been helpful over the years to have an extra man close by."

"I don't mind." Taima agreed. "Since my marriage, and now with the children I have had my brother, Kajika, come instead of me sometimes, and he will help with the extra work. There are other trusted men who can help when needed."

"Good." Said Samuel. "I'm worried they will try to hurt Ruth and her sons, to try to get some control over us and our activities here. As well as being worried about my niece, the set up at her farm is the best we have available for when several people have to be moved out of the county. If we lose the use of it, it will really harm our efforts."

"I agree, but my family is also at risk, and there is the continuing question of our cove. No one has been able to find it from the water without knowing right where it is, but if the wrong people find it from the land, it can be dangerous to all who use it." Peter added.

"I think our men can also keep an eye on Peter's family too. Daniel and Josh are the most at risk because they are in school, and are out in the community more, they are the easiest prey to attack. Our men can be around at the times when the boys are travelling to and from school." Siwili offered.

"Thank You God, for hiding Berry's Cove thus far." Samuel quickly prayed. "We must continue to protect it at any cost. I'm so glad it is right on your property Peter. Daniel and Josh are always telling me what a great fishing spot it is!"

"It is a good spot! I can tell you from experience, Kajika and I have been there many times with the boys. I think we can widen our range of protection to include the two families." Taima interjected.

The men continued talking and making plans for whatever trouble might come their way. Meanwhile, there were different serious discussions in the house.

When the two older little ones were settled and eating in the kitchen, the adult conversation continued in the living room with Aunt Elizabeth, Sarah, who was feeding Adam, and Ruth.

"I have always been concerned Martin would try to contact the boys at least, but I'd never considered the possibility of another family. My sons have siblings! I'd certainly never thought of that!" Ruth exclaimed.

"It's bigger than that dear." Aunt Elizabeth cautioned. "Martin's other family are very involved with the movement to stop our work helping the refugees. We may have to protect the boys from their siblings and their uncle. They might try to threaten to hurt the boys or you to encourage us to stop the work here."

"What a mess." Sarah added. "It's time now. I'm going out to hitch our horse to the wagon and leave to pick Josh and Daniel up from school. At least the snow has let up a bit. Can I leave Anna and Adam here?"

"Oh, Sarah, of course you can leave them here. I lost track of time. I'm so glad you remembered! Oh, Daniel, how will I tell him all about this mess?" Ruth answered.

When Sarah was dressed, she kissed Anna and Adam. She told them to be good for Auntie Elizabeth and Auntie Ruth and promised to return shortly with Josh and Daniel. "Okay Momma, Sammy and I are going to start new game with Shadow!" Anna answered; she and Sammy had really enjoyed playing together today, as hard as it was for the adults; the company for the youngest ones was a God send during this terrible snowstorm.

"No one expects you to be thinking of everything today, dear." Aunt Elizabeth said, as Sarah left the house. The thought of help telling Daniel soothed her nerves somewhat. "We'll all help you tell Daniel."

Siwili noticed Sarah as she was leaving the yard. "Where is your wife going Peter?"

"Oh, she must be on her way to pick the boys up from school." Peter answered. "I think I should go with her today." He leaped for the door to stop Sarah. Poking his face out the door, Peter hollered. "Sarah, wait for me!"

Quickly Peter dressed for the weather, and trudged through the snow to meet his wife at their wagon. The other men moved to the large window and watched in silence as the couple headed down the lane for the school in Sandwich Town.

The wind had died down and the snow let up. The peaceful and innocent snowy scene, of the couple in a horse-drawn sleigh leaving down the laneway however did not express the potential danger that now threatened the security of the activities in Sandwich and all of Essex County. The men watched the beautiful scene from the bunkhouse window and were left wondering just what the future held for them.

Daniel and Josh got to sing together during the School Christmas Concert which was held on the Friday night before Christmas. Uncle Samuel and Aunt Elizabeth came down for the performance and everyone had a wonderful evening.

The song the boys proudly sang was "**Go Tell It on the Mountain**". Their beautiful, clear youthful voices rang in praise of the birth of the Saviour:

1. While shepherds kept their watching o'er silent flocks by night,

Behold throughout the heavens there shone a holy light.

2. The shepherds feared and trembled when lo! Above the earth

Rang out the angel chorus that hailed our Saviour's birth.

3. Down in a lonely manger the humble Christ was born,

And God sent us salvation that blessed Christmas morn.

Chorus: Go tell it on the mountain, over the hills and everywhere,

Go tell it on the mountain that Jesus Christ was born.

The next morning, Saturday, they left for Amherstburg. They spent Sunday at the Methodist church in Amherstburg where Ruth grew up. Christmas Day was on Monday in 1843, and preparations were ready at the Patterson house for the celebrations. While they were gone, the community of Sandwich took shifts guarding the Logan Farm. Ruth and her family returned home in time for Daniel to return to school.

April 1844
CHAPTER 4

THE REST OF THE WINTER PASSED UNEVENTFULLY WITH THE people of the Band, and the residents of Sandwich and Amherstburg still watching for any signs of trouble from up London way. Daniel was still reeling from the information given to him that snowy afternoon about his father, and wondered about the siblings he and Sammy now knew they had in London. Sammy didn't fully understand all the details, after the revelations of that afternoon.

Now Daniel was better able to understand why the adults around him were concerned for their safety. He knew there were many people who were against helping the refugees and he remembered his father was one of those people. Now he knew the rest of his father's other family thought the same way.

On the second Saturday in April, there was still a cool nip in the air, but Daniel and Josh wanted to go fishing for the first time in this new season. Early in the morning, Daniel bundled up for the cold clammy air by the river, and left for Josh's house. As usual, he took the back way through the woods that bordered the two houses, and the path closest to the river. When he arrived, he called softly at Josh's kitchen door to pick him up; Josh met him at the door.

Quietly, so as not to wake the household, the boys then went to the barn to get their fishing poles and followed the well-worn path to their favorite spot in the cove. As they progressed further from Josh' house, they started talking excitedly, about the new season upon them. When they settled into their task of fishing, they found it was good today, and the company was even better.

Earlier in the winter, Scott and Peter promised this was the year they would take the two boys out and teach them to hunt deer. Part of the fun today, held the promise of new skills, and the responsibilities that come with this 'coming of age'.

When the boys felt they had enough fish for the two families, they headed back to Josh's house. His family were starting to move around outside. Peter waved at them from the barn where he was working, and Anna was out gathering eggs for breakfast. The boys dropped their poles off in the barn, and then went with Chance jumping at the fish, to the side of the barn to clean the fish for Josh's family. When the job was done, Josh brought his fish in the house, and Daniel headed home alone by the back way again with the fish for his family.

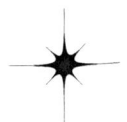

✦

"WHERE DID HE LEAVE THE PACKAGE?" The stranger hollered again at Ruth.

"I don't know what package you're talking about. Martin didn't leave anything here." Ruth and Sammy were tied by their hands and ankles to kitchen chairs by the two strangers who broke into the house earlier.

Shadow's angry barks and claws at the door of Sammy's room clamored in the background. The older and larger of the two men rooted through Ruth's, then Daniel's room and the guest room. He knocked on walls in the hallways, listening for hollow spots and possible hidden closets. He slammed cupboards and drawers in the kitchen looking for the mysterious 'package'.

"You — boy, your name is Sammy is it?" The larger man roared as he entered the kitchen and untied Sammy. Grabbing him by roughly by an arm he said: "Move your dog into another room. I want to look in the room where we put the dog."

When they got to Sammy's room, Sammy put Shadow in the guest room so the large man could search Sammy's room. "You know boy," He said quietly, lifting an eyebrow towards Sammy and nodding his head in a conspiratory way, he continued: "your Grandfather Logan has been wondering about you two boys for many years. He wants to see you. My friend and I would like to take you and your brother to see your grandfather; he is a very good man you know. You have a good dog here; we could take your dog too."

After he finished searching Sammy's room, Shadow was left in the guest room. The large man grabbed Sammy by his arm and led him back to the kitchen. On the way back he told Sammy:

"It's a secret, about us taking you and your brother to London to see your Grandfather, don't tell your mother." He roughly tied Sammy up again and went back to the living room to continue the search for the mysterious package.

Arriving at the end of the wood, Daniel was surprised to see two strange horses, and a quiet yard. The barn door was wide open, and the new wagon Mr. Burke delivered yesterday sat fully visible from where he stood. The door to the secret space in the wagon was open. Daniel was shocked. The barn door was never left open, especially when a wagon was there. It was too late in the morning for no one to be out tending the animals, and the cows were not out.

Daniel dropped his fish at the end of the wood, and ran back to Josh's house. Taima and Kajika were coming together today, but not until later in the morning.

"Something's wrong at my house!" He breathlessly hollered to Peter and Josh, who were both still working in the yard. "Everything's wrong," He halted for a breath. "Our animals aren't out in the yard, not even the cows. The barn door is open showing the new wagon and the opened secret compartment." He took another needed breath. "And there are strange horses in the yard. We are expecting Taima and Kajika later this morning, but the horses are not theirs."

"Josh I want you to go with Daniel to get the Sheriff and Mr. MacMillan." Said Peter. "I want you two boys to stay at the Blacksmith's Shop with Mr. MacMillan's father until I come for you. No arguments."

"Okay Poppa, come on Daniel, we'll use our horses." Said Josh as the two boys rushed for the barn to saddle some horses.

Sarah ran out to the yard when she heard the commotion. "Sarah, some strangers are at Ruth's place and I think they might want to take Daniel. If Josh is in the way, they'll take him too. You, Anna and Adam stay in the house until I come back, and keep the shotgun handy."

"Oh, yes, love, God is with you." Sarah answered.

Peter grabbed his rifle and went on foot to the Logan farm.

He stopped where Daniel dropped his fish, and everything was just as he reported. The barn door open with the wagon fully visible and the secret compartment to the wagon opened. There were strange horses tethered by the fence, and no one in the yard.

As Peter carefully inched his way closer to the house he heard Shadow barking and snarling loudly from one of the bedrooms in the house. He moved toward Ruth's kitchen and peeked in the window.

Ruth and Sammy were tied arms and feet to two of the kitchen chairs; they both looked terrified. Being still five and a half, Sammy didn't really fit the chair where he was tied. Peter noticed him trying to wiggle and find a more comfortable position. Peter thought Ruth might have seen him out of the corner of her eye, because he heard her say:

"Who are you people? Did Martin send you? My oldest son is gone for the whole day. Someone has to take care of my animals!"

Peter hadn't seen the men from last fall. "So," He thought, "these aren't the men from before. I wonder if they were hired by those two people, or are they from somewhere else. I can only see two men and two horses, but they might have someone else on look-out." Peter crept back toward the wood to keep an eye on the goings on, and wait for help.

✦

When the boys arrived at Sandwich Town, they tied the horses in front of the Blacksmith's shop and Daniel ran inside. Josh headed directly for the Sheriff's office.

As soon as Scott realized what Daniel was saying he started collecting his rifle, and gathering the things he needed for the trip to Ruth's farm. Daniel rattled on about joining the men to help. He worried about his mother and brother.

"Laddie," The elder MacMillan gently laid his hand on Daniel's shoulder. Daniel stopped talking and faced the kindly old man as he spoke softly to him, "I need you and Josh here while my son helps at your farm."

The men, in their discussions about the possibility of this happening, had already decided Daniel and Sammy should stay out of harm's way at Peter's or the MacMillan's shop. At this point, they couldn't get Sammy, but Daniel and Josh could stay here now. Daniel and Josh were together most of the time, and the men had also discussed the possibility of the strangers grabbing whoever was with the Logan children.

Just then Josh and the Sheriff burst into the shop.

"Are you ready Scott?" Scott nodded his head in reply. "Now Josh, we want you and Daniel to stay here and help Mr. MacMillan in the shop until we come for you. Let's go."

The boys' sullen attitudes reflected their thoughts on the decision the older men had made for them.

"Well, laddies," Angus MacMillan said quietly. "Bring your horses in the barn here, and then I have a job just suited for two strong young men. Join me in the back of the shop. We have some materials to be organized, and my son and I haven't had the time to do it ourselves."

The men had also decided they didn't want the boys to be readily seen through the window by anyone passing by the shop.

The Sheriff and Scott rode off on their horses towards the Logan farm.

They knew Peter would be there by now, and scouting for information. The two men decided to go directly down the lane toward the house, as if they were planning to see Ruth. As they approached Ruth's farm, they met Taima and Kajika, on the way to Ruth's lane.

The men from the Band explained they had made arrangements with Ruth and Daniel to come before lunchtime today and work, with Kajika coming back later to check on the families. The two men from Town brought Taima and Kajika up to date with the new developments.

They all decided to have the Band men enter the yard first, since they were expected in case anyone was watching from the house.

After they arrived in her yard, and tied their horses Kajika went directly in the barn to tend to the animals. By this time, the animals were loudly vocalizing their objections to being left alone for so long. They could also hear Shadow barking from inside the house.

Taima called out for Ruth as he wandered around the yard and looked for some sign of life. As he searched the ground, he could see men's footprints in the dirt from the horses leading in the house, but not leaving. Rounding the back of Ruth's house, he noticed Peter hiding by the end of the wood.

Gradually, he looked and stooped down as if finding more footprints in the dirt. Taima worked his way toward Peter, who had moved further out of sight.

Facing the wood, and standing in the line of sight of the house Taima spoke to Peter: "The Sheriff and Scott are at the end of the lane waiting for a sign from us." Taima told Peter without moving his head, in case he was being watched from the house.

"I have only seen two men, and they are both inside with Ruth and Sammy." Peter said. "I don't know if they have searched the barn and bunkhouse yet. When I got here the barn door was open, and the gate to the secret compartment in the wagon is opened, just like it is now. Ruth and Sammy are each tied to a chair in the kitchen."

"Shadow is going to beat down that door himself if this goes on much longer!" Taima smiled. "I don't want to be around those men when he gets loose! I'm going back to the yard and help my brother." said Taima. "We will go about our business as usual. The Sheriff and Scott are waiting at the main road; you can meet up with them there."

"Okay, I'm off now, I'm hoping we can just capture them, find out who sent them and what they want."

Peter went deeper into the wood to circle the farm and double back to the main road where the Sheriff and Scott were awaiting word.

Back at the main road, Peter startled the two men when he burst through the wood ahead of them.

"Thanks for coming." Peter said. "How are Josh and Daniel?"

"Okay, they're with my father." Said Scott. "As we planned, he is keeping them busy at the back of the shop. Where are Sarah, and the two little ones?"

"I told Sarah to stay in the house with the children and to keep her shotgun handy." Peter answered. "I ran into Taima at the farm, Kajika is working as if nothing were wrong. Taima wandered around the yard as if looking for some sign of the family. We met in the wood and he told me you were here.

"Ruth and Sammy are tied to two chairs in the kitchen and I have only seen two men. They didn't come out when the men from the Band approached, it seems they plan to lay low and wait for Daniel. I think Ruth saw me looking in the kitchen window because she loudly asked who they were, and told them her oldest son would be gone all day. I think they are not the same men as before. By the way, Shadow is locked in one of the bedrooms I think. He is loud, and very angry."

"Well." The Sheriff smiled and said. "Scott, I think it's time we went to the house to call on Ruth, and see what happens. Now that we have Shadow and some reinforcements in place, it's time to take our stand."

"I agree Sheriff." Answered Scott, smiling.

"I'll stay close in the bush in case you need me." Said Peter as he crept back into the wood.

Shortly, the Sheriff and Scott could hear Shadow's angry barking as they approached the house. They smiled at each other as they started knocking at Ruth's front door. Taima and Kajika met them at the door by the second knock. "We haven't seen anyone yet this morning, and that's unusual. Shadow's really upset, and there's usually someone about." He said innocently.

"Taima, why don't you and Scott go around to the back door?" The Sheriff suggested. "Kajika and I will wait for you to enter and then come in by the front here."

✦

"Look Momma! There's the light from the other side of the river that speaks to Poppa!"

Eight year old Anna was so happy to see the signal; it had been such a boring day for her since the outside work was done. Sarah would not let her and Adam outside to play with Chance. They finished the most necessary outside chores, and then holed up in the house, waiting for word from Peter.

She, Anna and Adam had been praying for Peter, Josh, and Ruth and her boys all day. Not wanting to frighten the little ones, Sarah told them they had to pray that Poppa and the boys 'special task' today would go well.

"Oh dear, there's people coming tonight." Sarah ran for their signal light to answer. The reply would tell her how many people were coming across tonight. After she answered and got her reply, she told the children they would have to pray again, so Poppa and the boys could finish their 'special task' in time to help with tonight's new arrivals.

✦

61

"Hi Angus." Seamus from the General Store just dropped in the Blacksmith's shop. "Bessie threw her shoe this morning while I was out delivering some goods. If you're not too busy, I wonder if you can take care of her soon."

"Sure Seamus, did you see my son and the Sheriff around Ruth's farm while you were about?"

"No, I didn't go that way. I went in the other direction towards Assumption Church." Seamus answered. "What's going on there?"

"There are some strangers at Ruth's place. Peter sent Josh and Daniel here to get help and I have the two lads in the back here working. They think Martin's friends from London are up to no good again. I'm thinking there might be more trouble than they're ready to handle. Do you think you can gather a small posse to follow them? I wonder if you can also check on Sarah at their farm, she and the little ones are all alone."

"Sure Angus, I'll go to Sara's house myself. I'll get a few good men together to see if they need help at Ruth's place. Can I borrow one of your horses and leave my Bessie with you?"

"Sure Seamus, take Master, I can get to your Bessie later this morning."

Seamus left after switching the horses to gather some help for his new job.

✦

The curtains were drawn in the kitchen, but Scott and Taima could see Ruth and Sammy tied to the chairs, they couldn't see anyone else.

"Ruth!" Scott hollered as he shouldered the latched door open. "What's going on?"

"Stop there!" Threatened one of the captors as he held a rifle directly at Scott's head.

Just then, the Sheriff and Kajika both carrying rifles burst in from the front door. They surprised the older and larger man who also had a rifle. Kajika was able to disarm him before he could get it aimed at either of them. Taima jumped in the kitchen after Scott and grabbed the gun from the man who had him.

The sudden commotion started Shadow on a new round of angry barks and snarls and jumps at the door. The Sheriff and Kajika hustled the second man into the kitchen. Quickly, the four men successfully captured the two captors.

"Let me untie these ropes." Scott told Sammy as he pulled at the knots on Sammy's wrists and ankles. Sammy immediately ran to his room to rescue Shadow. Then the real commotion began! Taima untied Ruth's bonds, but almost before she was free Shadow and then Sammy lunged into her arms. Ruth held Sammy for a long time, and asked: "Where is Daniel?"

There was no immediate answer to Ruth's question because Shadow, now ten months old, and close to eighty pounds had moved his attention to jump on the interlopers. From one to the other he kept knocking each man down. The rescuers kept pulling them up, but just as they were trying to move the handcuffed men, Shadow would knock them down again. Finally the men were left on the floor until Shadow was contained by Ruth.

"Daniel and Josh are safe with my father." Scott finally assured Ruth.

"I heard all the commotion that was quick work!" Peter said as he entered through the kitchen door. "Awe, Scott! What did you do to this latch?"

"Then don't look at the front latch." Kajika advised Peter.

Once he had full control of the two strangers, Sheriff Pollard asked the men: "Who sent you?"

"We were told this woman hides slaves." The larger man snarled at him, "We saw that special wagon she has too, so we know it's true. My boss says she is keeping his two grandsons from him, and training them to help her. We were sent to save the boys from her and take them back to their grandfather."

"Are you alone down here?" The Sheriff asked them.

"Yes, but if we aren't back in London by tomorrow, he'll send some others after us." The other man answered.

"That's it." The Sheriff said. "Let's get them to jail for now. Taima can you help Scott and me take them in? I will have to get more information from these two. I don't think we are done with the people from London."

"Kajika will you please stay and keep watch for Ruth and Sammy for a while?" Scott asked. "After we drop off these two at the jail, I'd like to pick up Josh and Daniel from my father's place and bring them home."

"No problem Scott. We still have lots more work to do here anyway." Kajika said.

"I'd appreciate that Scott." Peter added, "I would like to check on Sarah, Anna and Adam. I agree with you Sheriff. I really don't believe these two are alone."

Ruth watched as the Sheriff, Scott and Taima led her two captors down the lane for jail, and Peter left for home. She thanked God Daniel had the presence of mind to go for help instead of trying to help her and Sammy himself. "God has really granted my son with wisdom beyond his years." She thought.

✦

"Here comes Mr. Murphy from the General Store Momma!" Anna was so excited to see another change in the boring environment of the day!

Sarah ran to answer the door before Seamus arrived on the porch. "Hi Seamus, did you hear anything from Ruth's farm?"

"Not yet Sarah, I just heard from Angus MacMillan that something was going on." Sarah let him in the door as he continued talking. "He sent me here to tell you Josh and Daniel are safe with him. He also had me send a posse on to Ruth's farm in case the men need help there. I wanted to come here to see if you needed help, Angus said you were alone."

"I just got a signal from Detroit saying four people are coming here tonight and Peter doesn't know yet. What a time; we don't know if we are even safe here now." Sarah was uneasy at the prospect of people arriving here to find more danger.

Adam ran squealing over to Seamus. He was excited to see new company. Seamus obliged the boy by picking him up with a flourish and then held him close.

"Hi little man!" He said to Adam, to Sarah he said: "We'll figure it out somehow Sarah." Seamus assured her. "Remember, we are doing the right thing. We are following the law by helping the refugees, and they are not."

Just then Peter entered by the back door; he had taken the foot path home. Adam immediately lost interest in Seamus, wiggled and cried: "Poppa!" When Seamus put him down Adam made a bee line for his father, but Anna beat him.

"Ruth and Sammy are safe! Two men were holding them hostage in the house and we got them!" Peter hollered while walking from the kitchen to the sitting room.

"Hi son!" He said as he scooped the running child up in his arms and hugged Anna. "The Sheriff, Scott and Taima are taking the two men to jail now! They wanted to kidnap Ruth's boys and take them to London!" He stopped short when he saw Seamus. "Seamus, what brings you here? Is everything okay?"

"Everything's fine. Angus was worried Sarah needed some help here. We also sent a posse on the way to Ruth's house, in case extra help was needed there."

"They might cross paths!" Peter grinned. "But we are worried those two are not alone, it might be prudent to have some people search the area."

"You're right about that Peter." Seamus agreed "Sarah got a signal from Detroit saying some people are crossing the river tonight, and we have to make sure they are safe."

"Anna saw the signal light before me." Sarah added. "I answered, and they signaled back there would be four people. We were worried you would not be back in time to help, and there might be danger for the refugees."

"We were praying for you and Josh and your special task today Poppa, where's Josh?" Anna asked.

"Mr. MacMillan has gone to pick him and Daniel up from the Blacksmith's Shop sweetheart, he'll be home soon. Seamus, I think I can handle things here for now, would you please try to contact the posse and see if they can start looking for more strangers in the area?"

"Sure thing Peter, I'm glad things worked out at Ruth's place. Now we just have to keep it safe here for tonight." Seamus answered, relieved for the safety thus far, but knowing it was not over yet.

★

He heard the horse come in through the stables, and knew Scott was home. Angus waited until Scott entered the Blacksmith shop from the back.

"Well boys, how is the work going? Did my Poppa keep you busy?"

"How are my Momma and Sammy?" A worried Daniel questioned him.

"Everyone is fine, but two men from London had them tied up in the kitchen. Shadow was causing quite a commotion. Someone locked him in one of the bedrooms and he just kept barking and jumping at the door! If he ever got loose, the men would have run for sure!"

"Wow Daniel," Josh chimed in. "I bet Chance would have been just as brave! Can we go home yet?"

"Yes, I think so; I'm here to take both of you home now."

Angus MacMillan entered from the shop door.

"Poppa! Did these lads I left you today do a good job?"

"Aye my Laddie, they're right good workers, even though they were both worried about their families."

"If you can spare them now, I think I'll take them home Poppa. Lads, would you please get our wagon ready to leave? I'll be there shortly." When the boys left for the stable, he told his father.

"The Sheriff has the two men in jail now. We met the posse you and Seamus arranged on the way to town. Thank you by the way, and Taima, who was with us, went back to Ruth's farm to help his brother.

"There were two men who tied Ruth and Sammy up in the kitchen and were waiting for Daniel to come home. We think they were trying to kidnap Daniel and Sammy to take to Martin, even though they said it was for his father. They insist they haven't seen Martin either."

Thoughtfully, he added. "Maybe Martin really left to go out west. They also told us there were more people coming if they didn't return with the boys. We are concerned they might have more men from London in the area now. Martin's other family has had all winter to plan for this."

"Oh Laddie, I agree; I fear there's more coming." The elder MacMillan returned.

"That's right Poppa; I fear we've just started this fight. I'll be off with the boys now. I'll try to be home soon, but I want to spend some time with Ruth first, just to make sure she's okay."

"She's a good woman son, and she's free to marry now."

"Poppa…" Scott had been thinking about talking with Ruth, he just had to think of a good time.

✦

Ruth walked through her house, touching her furniture, caressing the blanket she knitted to throw on the chesterfield. Things looked normal, but everything was different now. Strangers had been here and had invaded her home; threatened her family, and sense of security.

They had searched every inch of her house, saying they were looking for a package Martin should have for them. She had seen nothing out of the ordinary over all the years he was gone. She didn't remember him having a package with him when he left, only his saddlebags.

The men didn't seem to find what they were looking for either. By the time the rescuers arrived her captors were getting angry with her answers, and Sammy's crying. She didn't understand what the people from London were talking about when they asked about a package.

Sammy and Shadow were outside 'helping' Taima and Kajika with the animals in the yard. Sammy was clingy to her for about a half an hour, but was now clinging to them.

She couldn't wait for Scott to return with Daniel, but she was having trouble holding her emotions together. Could she really keep her sons safe from these people? Just how much did Martin have to do with what was going on now? They said they were looking for him too, but Martin lied, are they lying too? Where did Martin go, and what is in this mysterious package he was supposed to have for them?

✦

"Scott! I'm glad you came so quickly with Josh and Daniel!" Peter was happy and relieved they were back. "Seamus has gone to ask the posse to check for strangers around this area. There are four new people coming tonight! We need to know things are safe for their arrival."

"Oh Peter! Wow." He paused. "Tonight?"

On one hand Scott was glad to hear this. Ruth would have something different to think about, other than her problems from today. On the other hand, there might still be danger in the area. "I came here first to drop off Josh, then I was going spend some time with Ruth just to make sure she will be okay. I'd also like to ask Taima if he would send someone to Amherstburg to tell Samuel and Elizabeth what has happened here today."

"Good idea Scott, we've been consumed here with planning for the safety of the new people coming over here tonight. We haven't had a chance to think of Ruth's family in Amherstburg."

"Oh dear Peter, before Scott and Daniel leave, let's just have a prayer thanking Our Lord for our safety today. Also for Samuel and Elizabeth, Ruth and her boys, and for the work we must do tonight." Sarah gathered her children and Daniel together so they could all participate and agree in prayer.

Scott led first: "Dear Father in heaven, thank you for the safety we enjoyed this morning, and thank you for your assistance in safely arresting the people who threatened our Sister-In-Christ and her son. Be in our midst tonight as we do your will in helping four more people to escape from slavery."

"Yes Lord." Peter added. "Thank you for Daniel's wisdom beyond his years in seeking help for his mother and brother, and thank you for helping us arrive in time to rescue them. I also ask you for your assistance this evening with this new task before us. Once again Dear Lord, we ask You to protect the safety of our Cove."

"Thank you Lord for helping me see the light that talks to my Poppa, and help Poppa and the others do their special task tonight." Anna added.

"Thank you Lord for helping us protect my mother and Sammy from those bad people, who tried to hurt us today." Daniel's prayer was simple and earnest.

"Thank you Lord, for Uncle Scott and his father who helped us today, and thank you for my Poppa and our Sheriff and our friends Taima and Kajika and all the others who helped us stay safe today." Josh agreed.

"Thank you Lord, for my family, and my friends in this community and for all the work you have allowed us to accomplish thus far. Send your angels to guard us tonight, as you have so many times before. We are grateful for every time You help us with Your work in this area." Sarah held Adam close to her for the prayer and he quietly listened to the prayers of the others. "We ask that you comfort our Sister-In-Christ this day, and steel her for Your work ahead."

After the prayer, Scott and Daniel left quickly for Ruth's house.

"Here they come down the lane Momma!" Sammy yelled from the yard. "Daniel, wow you missed what happened here today Shadow is so brave!"

"I heard Sammy, Uncle Scott told me how brave Shadow was today. You and Momma were brave too. Josh and I went to get Uncle Scott and the Sheriff; we were worried about you." Daniel ran to hug his mother.

"Momma, I was worried about you. I'm glad they got those men who tied you and Sammy up. Were those men really sent by my Grandfather?"

"The men said your Grandfather Logan sent them, because he thinks I'm not taking care of you and Sammy properly." Ruth carefully answered Daniel.

Kajika and Taima joined the gathering in the yard between the barn and Ruth's house to welcome Daniel. "Good work Daniel!" Taima thumped Daniel's shoulder in praise. "You really saved your family by getting help for them."

"Good job Daniel!" Kajika chimed in.

"Ruth, there is a posse looking for more strangers in the area, but when we got to Peter's house to drop off Josh, we found out Sarah received a signal from Detroit saying four people are coming across the river tonight." Scott said.

"How much work do you have left here Taima?" Scott said. "I was wondering if you could leave now. Daniel and I can finish up here. We need to ask the Band for help tonight and we need someone to travel to Amherstburg to tell Samuel and Elizabeth what has been going on here today."

"We are done here now Scott, Kajika and I were talking about telling Mr. and Mrs. Patterson after we leave here today. We were planning to take a short cut we know straight through to the Patterson farm so we could be home in good time tonight. If you are going to need help with security for the new arrivals tonight we will change our plans. I can go directly to Amherstburg, and Kajika can go home and tell our people about the crossing tonight."

"I think we are going to need all the help we can get tonight with security Taima, I'd appreciate your help." Scott said.

"We'll leave now then." Taima said. "I'll go to Amherstburg and Kajika; you go directly to tell our people. I'm glad everything turned out well for you and your sons Ruth."

"Sure Taima, I hope things work out this well tonight too." Added Kajika.

After their good friends from the Band left, Scott took Ruth by the hand and said:

"Ruth, I want to look around the barn and bunkhouse to see if those men bothered anything we will need tonight. Do you want to help me check things out?"

"Oh yes Scott, I need to get out of the house; I've been feeling uncomfortable in my own home. Those men went all through my things." Ruth answered him. She was still shaken up from this morning's threat to her and her children. "Boys, why don't you come with us, I'd like you to stay near me." There was no argument from either of the boys.

While the boys walked ahead of them, with Shadow close at their side, Scott took Ruth's arm in his as she quietly told him about the men searching her house. "Those men were searching for a package from Martin. They seemed to be sure they would find something here and they are certain Martin would not leave without sending them this important package."

"I'm going to tell Sheriff Pollard in the morning. We are busy with the new refugees tonight; he can ask the prisoners about the package tomorrow. I wonder what is in this mysterious package."

✦

After nightfall Anna and Adam were down for the night, and Peter, Sarah, Scott and Josh sat at the kitchen table looking out the big window over Berry's Cove and into the main stream of the Detroit River.

"Here they come!" Josh was excited; this was the first time his parents let him stay up for the expected travellers.

"Son, I want you to come down with Scott and me tonight. You're big enough to help with the landing. Just do what we tell you; tonight we need you to keep an eye out for trouble from the land."

"Yes, Poppa I'll make you proud tonight." Josh's pride in his father's confidence in him overflowed in his spirit. He wanted to do the best job he could tonight.

They had seen activity all night long; men from the Band, and some local workers in the cause, patrolling the area on and surrounding Peter's farm. Some men were riding on horseback and some men were on foot hiding in the nearby woods. Everyone was watching for strangers who might try to start trouble.

Jackson, and the Hubbs brothers, Hank and Abe, were watching Ruth's farm for any sign of trouble. Earlier, Scott and Ruth had not found anything disturbed around the secret places in the bunkhouse or the hiding place in the hayloft of the barn. They figured the men from London didn't get any further than the wagon in the barn with their search of the farmyard buildings.

This afternoon Ruth told Scott about the search of her house, no secret passageways had been built in the house. At least they didn't think the strangers were aware of the secret passageways to and from the barn and the bunkhouse. The new people would be brought to her farm by way of the back path. That way was being watched closely by local helpers and the volunteers from the Band to keep it safe.

In Ruth's house, Amitola, Siwili and Maka's daughter and Apenimon's sister, and long-time friend of Ruth was keeping her company. When Amitola heard what happened at the farm this morning, she insisted Ruth should not be alone on this first night. Especially with new people coming tonight and the extra work which came with them.

The two women sat in the living room of Ruth's home, Ruth knitting, and Amitola working on a weaving project while they talked and waited for the travellers.

"I'm so grateful for your coming here tonight Amitola. The nights we have new people coming are always stressful, but I am especially upset tonight. The search the men did of my house has really upset my sense of security I'm shaking with every move I make. They've handled my personal things, my clothing. They searched Daniel's room, Sammy's room and then made Sammy move Shadow into the guest room while they searched Sammy's room. They searched all through the living room and the kitchen, knocking on walls and thumping floors for a secret hiding place."

"What were they searching for in the house Ruth?"

"Some mysterious package they are sure Martin had for them. They're boss is sure he would not have just left without bringing it to them."

"We know you are worried Ruth, that's why I'm here. My people are with all the other neighbours around here looking out for strangers who might try to make trouble tonight. We are trying to make things as safe as possible for you and your sons, the Berry family, as well as the new arrivals." Amitola assured Ruth.

Sammy was sent to bed, but Daniel, also was allowed to stay up that night. He was being trained to be the official welcome person at the bunkhouse. Jackson stayed at the house to show Daniel his new duties. At Ruth's place they always made sure clean sheets were on the bunks, and towels for baths and clean clothes if they were needed, were ready for the new people.

Later, while Ruth and Amitola prepared the food for the refugees' first warm meal in Canada, Daniel and Jackson would show the people around the bunkhouse, and later carry water for baths. When the new people were ready to eat, Daniel would help Jackson bring the repast to the bunkhouse. That night's landing and travel to Ruth's bunkhouse went as planned and was safe for everyone concerned.

Early the next morning, Sunday, Josh and Daniel swelled with pride while sitting and fishing at their spot in the cove. The fishing was good, but they spent most of their time remembering their part in helping the night before.

About the same time the boys were fishing two members of the Band arrived at Ruth's farm to use the wagon to carry the four travellers to safety. The new people were safe, and so were the residents of the Sandwich community.

Ruth, Sarah and Peter had decided to skip church this morning; they felt it was not safe to leave their homes with the threat of strangers in the vicinity. The woods surrounding the two farms were still being watched by friends in the community, as well as extra help for the travellers.

The two families had sent word to their church homes to pray for them and the safety of the whole community. Amitola decided to stay another day to help Ruth with the daily chores; Ruth was still shaky from the day before. Amitola thought she could be a calming influence on Ruth, Daniel and Sammy.

Everyone in the Berry and Logan households enjoyed the fresh fish provided by Josh and Daniel for the noon meal. Later, Daniel and Sammy worked together at the outside chores and Amitola and Ruth did the extra laundry from the visitors in the bunkhouse last night.

Earlier in the morning before the regular services at the Sandwich Methodist Church, Scott paid a visit to Sheriff Pollard at St. John's Anglican Church.

"Hi Richard, yesterday while I was helping to check out Ruth's farm after everyone left, she told me those two men searched her house, every room, and drawer in the place. They were pounding walls, and looking for a secret hiding place and for that mysterious package everyone keeps talking about. Ruth is very upset, she doesn't know or remember Martin having anything, and she is feeling violated by the search."

"Those two men last fall were talking about a package too." The Sheriff replied. "Later, when I get back to check on them in the jail, I'll try to find out if they know what is supposed to be in the package."

Ruth and Sarah and Peter decided to keep Daniel, Josh and Anna from school on Monday. The adults needed a chance to talk to the children about what was going on at their homes and how much to say to people at school and in town. Daniel and Josh knew some, but had to be brought up to date on the new information. The adults had to impress on Anna and Sammy especially not to mention Berry's Cove at all to outsiders.

Under The North Star

Early Monday morning the original strangers from last fall again came to town and checked in with Philip at the Post Office before they made arrangements for a place to stay. Seamus noticed them enter the building and decided this would be a good time to stock up on stamps for the store.

He quietly entered the anteroom of the Post Office while a spirited conversation was in progress between one of the strangers and Philip, the Postmaster. He listened quietly on the other side of the door separating the anteroom from the office.

"I don't know how all those people found out about what you were doing at the house on Saturday Mr. Johnson." Philip stated. "They don't confide in me around here."

"You are getting paid well to let us know what's going on." David Johnson roared. "Has anyone said anything about Martin? I can't believe he left here altogether and didn't tell his father where he was going. Charles wants to see his grandsons; that woman can't have them all to herself."

"Martin left town, before I came here. No one seems to know anything about where he went. I did hear that they found out about John's sister, Martin's real wife. You won't be able to get any of Samuel Patterson's money or land through Ruth now." Philip told him.

Seamus quietly left the anteroom the way he came and went directly to the Sheriff's office.

"We have another problem Sheriff." Seamus told him. "Has anyone come yet to see the new prisoners?"

"Not yet, I filed the papers, and sent them in Saturday night's mail pouch, the judge should be in town on Thursday to see them. The men said someone would be looking for them by today if they were not back in London last night."

"I saw those two from last fall go into the Post Office this morning. While listening at the anteroom door I just heard Philip talking to David Johnson and John Daily. They were discussing Saturday's events at Ruth's house. David was very angry, and he reminded Philip he was getting paid to report to him."

"Philip is getting paid to report to him!" The Sheriff added.

Seamus continued. "David also said he was representing Martin's father. They are still looking for Martin. They don't believe Martin would

73

leave without telling them where he was going. As well, Samuel's investigator was right. They are actively looking for a way to control Samuel's money and holdings. Philip also told them we found out about Martin's real wife and his children with her."

"This is going to get uglier." The Sheriff stated. "Thanks for letting me know, I guess we found our information leak in this area. I'm glad Philip never really involved himself with what is going on with the refugees here, but he still could have heard quite a bit. I'm assuming David has come here to see the men we have here now."

"Should I send word to Ruth?"

"Not right now, nothing will happen with the two men here until the Judge comes. I want to see if I can get more information from David and possibly have more information to pass along. Good thing we've been keeping the guards up at Ruth's property. Thanks for telling me what you heard."

"Okay," Seamus answered. "I have to get back to my store for now."

"Come back here a little after you see them leave my office, I might have a message for Ruth." The Sheriff replied thoughtfully.

Mary Anne had been keeping watch over her husband's movements between their customers' visits since he left the store. The store was empty of customers when he returned. After filling her in on his findings, they decided to take turns watching the Sheriff's office so Seamus could return after David and John left the Sheriff's office.

Soon they noticed David and John, travel from the Post Office to the Public House the same place they stayed last fall. After spending a short time at the Public House, the two men went to the Sheriff's Office. They stayed in the Sheriff's Office for about an hour, and then went back to the Public House. Seamus waited until he thought they would stay there for a while and then went across to the Sheriff's Office.

"Well, what do we do now?" He asked the Sheriff.

"David Johnson pretended he didn't know we found out about Martin's real wife, and tried to assert some authority over Ruth and her children on behalf of Martin's father. I told him Ruth was told by Martin his family was from Toronto and she didn't expect any letters from London. I also reminded him Ruth and Martin's marriage was not legal.

I told him that Ruth stated Martin's family had never reached out to her at all, nor had they ever reached out to her sons until David and John came sneaking around last fall. Last fall they were secretive and didn't tell her who they were or what they wanted. I told him that trying to have those men kidnap the children on Saturday was no way for a grandfather to meet his grandsons.

"I also told him we were guarding Ruth and her property. If anyone tries to go near her, her sons or her property again they would end up in jail, just like these two. David tried to bail these two out of jail, but I told him they would have to stay until the judge came on Thursday and he will make a decision."

"Well, do you think they will stay away from Ruth and her boys?"

"I don't know. Could you get word to Ruth and the Berry's not to let Daniel or the Berry children go school without an adult present. As well they will have to stay close to home where we can watch them. Those people from out of town must realize the two families are close." the Sheriff answered Seamus.

"Sure, I think I'll take Scott with me and we can tell her and the boys together and assure them we will be still keeping an eye on them."

"Thanks Seamus, by the way, Scott told me the men searched Ruth's house while they had her and Sammy tied up the other day. They were looking for that package these two were talking about last fall. Tell Scott, no one is telling me what was in the package. Keep me posted." The Sheriff replied.

✦

Later, at Ruth's farm, Amitola was just getting ready to leave for home when Scott and Seamus arrived at her door. Ruth was cautious as she welcomed the men in for tea.

"Amitola, could you please stay a little longer?" She could see the worry in the faces of the men.

"Yes, of course Ruth, something tells me they have some information I should pass on to my people."

"Your right, Amitola," Scott said. "We have news from the Sheriff."

"Yes," Seamus added. "David Johnson and John Daily, the men who came here last fall, came to Town this morning and visited Philip at the Post office. By the way, we found out Phillip has been reporting to the people from London."

"I've met Philip from the Post Office." Amitola interjected. "He comes out of the building when my people are in town to talk to us. He has a superior attitude about him and mostly asks us what we are doing in Town, as if we would never have any business there. We don't trust him."

75

"I remember when I received the first letter from London." Ruth remembered. "I didn't really know him then, he said all the right things to me, but I didn't trust his attitude. I'm glad I have never said anything about what we do for the cause."

"Is there any more information you would have me pass on to my people?" Amitola said. "I must be getting home to my family."

"There's the obvious problem of being more careful about what Philip can see or hear. Other than that we haven't had a chance to make formal plans for this new development. I think we should keep close watch on both Ruth's boys and the Berry children. Sammy hasn't started school yet, so he will be with Ruth, but Daniel and Josh go out on their own now, and should be watched more closely. Anna has started school and I think she is at risk too. Mostly, we should keep close watch on these two farms, and protect Berry's Cove." Seamus said.

"Seamus is right." Scott said. "The Sheriff wanted us to assure you Ruth, we would be keeping watch for you and your boys. But more importantly, he also wants to keep watch on the whole community who are helping the refugees. These people from London want to shut down our project. I think we should all keep our eyes out for any strangers who might jeopardize the cause."

"I think I know what to tell my people." Amitola said. "Especially about Philip, we will continue keeping watch on the area. Send us word when you need help again."

The men and Ruth walked Amitola out to the barn to collect her horse.

"Thank you for coming to help and to stay with me these last two nights Amitola." Ruth said as the two women hugged. "God grant you travel mercies on your way home."

"Be safe, my sister." Amitola waved as she called back while she mounted her horse to leave.

As they watched Amitola head down the path for the main road, Scott asked: "Ruth, where is Daniel right now?"

Ruth smiled at him. "Guess! He and Josh HAD to go fishing again this morning! This is three days in a row! They are so proud they were allowed to help on Saturday night, I'm sure there is more reliving their experiences than actual fishing going on there! Besides, Daniel lost his fish on Saturday when he dropped them in the woods; he actually went to find them and discovered the local wildlife had a feast; only scales and some of the bones were left! I guess they're still trying to make up for the lost fish."

"Oh, right!" Scott laughed. "I'm going to see Peter and then to the cove. Seamus, can you stay here until Taima or Kajika comes if I'm not back soon? I have to tell Peter, and Sarah, what's going on in Town. We also have to make sure the boys fully understand why they can't talk to Philip."

"I can stay for a while Scott. I think I'll help Ruth talk to Sammy also; we can't risk him saying too much when he's in Town. He, Anna and Adam are around here, and they all hear much more than we know. Adam is starting to talk now, and is very vulnerable."

"You're right Seamus, I'll talk to Peter and Sarah about it, Anna's attending school now, and Sammy will be soon. I'm taking the back way."

Seamus and Ruth called Sammy from his game with Shadow. They tried to carefully explain that because the people who tied them up were trying to steal him and Daniel from Ruth, he must be very careful not to repeat anything the adults said to each other. They told him that except for Ruth or the few other adults they named to him, he was to repeat nothing to anyone.

Sammy shuffled his feet and looked at the ground. He sneaked glances at Seamus and his mother then back at the ground while he listened to Seamus talk.

"Mr. Murphy." Sammy slowly spoke while continuing to study the dirt at his feet. "Should I tell you something somebody else told me not to tell you?" Ruth and Seamus looked at each other, surprised.

Carefully, Ruth asked him: "Who told you a secret sweetheart?"

"The man who made me move Shadow from my room to the guest room." Sammy answered, still studying the dirt.

"Please tell us sweetheart." Ruth begged.

"The man said Shadow is a good dog, and when they took Daniel and me to see Grandfather Logan they were going to take Shadow too. He's right Momma, Shadow is a good dog.

"I've never seen my Grandfather Logan, the man said he is really nice, and he wants to see me and Daniel." He was a little hesitant in adding. "I'd like to see him, Momma but only with you."

Seamus bent down to Sammy's level and carefully cupped his hands under Sammy's chin, and tipped his face up to his own and studied Sammy's eyes. "Thank you for telling us Sammy that was the right thing to do. I think that man is not a good man Sammy." Seamus said gently.

"Those two men frightened you and your mother. Nice men wouldn't have tied you up, and they wouldn't have been carrying guns and threatening the men who came to your rescue.

"If your Grandfather Logan wants to see you and Daniel, he should just ask your mother, that man is lying to you. Nobody can take you from your mother without her permission, they want to hurt you and Daniel and your mother."

Sammy hung his head sadly. "I guess I knew it all the long. Is my Grandfather Logan a bad man too? I hear people say my Poppa was a bad man."

Ruth joined Seamus at Sammy's eye level and answered him. "We don't know that Sammy, but Grandfather Logan is not trying to see you in a friendly way."

Ruth didn't know how much he had heard her say, and didn't know what to tell him about his father. "As far as your Poppa, I just think he just wasn't happy here, and left."

The conversations at the cove and the Berry's home were less revealing. Daniel, Josh, Anna and Adam had never met the men who had broken into Ruth's house.

✦

Ruth woke up slowly to the early morning calling of local birds. It was the perfect way to awaken, she thought. As she lay quietly in her bed she listened carefully, and soon heard the soft rustle of the branches in the surrounding trees in the lazy early morning spring breeze. The buds were starting to show, but no leaves yet. She knew it was time to get up and start the day, but she just wanted to stay and relax in the calm of this early morning a little longer.

It was still a task to finally get up and face the day, she was thankful Amitola was able to stay with her those first two nights. It was comforting to know her friends and neighbours were watching out for trouble at the farm and the surrounding areas. Most of all she knew, sure, there was a threat to her, also to the whole area, but she wasn't alone.

Martin's family and friends from London wanted to stop the work they were doing to help the refugees. This pro-slavery attitude was behind all the trouble, she realized her family and her were only a part of their larger plan. This distorted thinking was the only reason Martin came down to Essex County in the first place, and it was why the people from London continued to cause trouble. It was hard for her to face the truth; Martin was just using her as a means to reach his final goal.

She and her sons probably meant nothing to Martin or the people in London. The men who were arrested trying to kidnap them were in jail now; she really didn't think they would try anything big until those men were free. Maybe after a trial they would have to spend some more time in jail for what they did to her and Sammy.

She had always viewed her sons, as a gift from God. But now, especially after this last winter, and spring the gift of Daniel and Sammy shone more brightly. For all the suffering that resulted from Martin and his plans; her two sons were most wonderful boys. They were smart, inquisitive, and talented, each son possessed gifts from Our Loving Father in heaven.

Daniel loved to sing. He had taken up playing the guitar and was starting to write songs to sing in church, and at community gatherings. Sammy, was practicing his whittling with Jackson, and was getting really good at it. He also started drawing local scenery and even some people. Both boys had a sweet spirit about them, their love for God was revealed in the way they treated the people around them. Who knows where each of these gifts will lead?

Aloud Ruth said to God: "I commit my life, and my sons to You Dear Lord. Let each day from now on be Your day. Show me how to act, and not react; show me what You would have me do each day. Dear Lord let me rest in the loving palms of Your Hands from this day until You call me home to be with You. Guide my sons, who love and trust You each day, to hunger for more knowledge of You, and to follow Your Word and Your plan for their lives."

April, 1845
CHAPTER 5

"Anna!" Josh called, "Anna, where are you?"

"She was just here, following us!" Daniel wondered. "Here comes Kajika, now. Kajika! We lost Anna!"

"Why are you out of school so soon?" Kajika called back.

"Our teacher, Miss Temple, had to leave school early for an emergency and she sent us students home. I guess we should have gone to Uncle Scott's shop and wait there for you." Daniel replied; as he held Sammy's hand a little tighter. It was Sammy's first year of school.

"Yes, I want you three boys to head back to the Blacksmith's shop now. Where was Anna when you saw her last?" Kajika said.

"We were waiting in front of the school for you, but decided to start home alone. Anna was talking with some of her friends by the front door, and we called her to follow us home." Josh said, "She said she was coming right behind us."

"I saw her start towards us." Daniel added hesitantly."

"You head to the Blacksmith's shop right now and tell Mr. MacMillan what happened so we can get started on our search for Anna." Kajika instructed the boys. "Tell him I am going back to the school and ask around and look for signs of Anna."

The three boys headed for the Blacksmith Shop in Town quickly, while Kajika headed back for the one-room schoolhouse attended by the local children.

Kajika arrived at the schoolhouse quickly and approached three young friends of Anna's.

"Hi girls, did you see where Anna Berry went?" He asked.

"Her brother called her to follow him, but a white man came up in a carriage and talked to her. She went with him." Jennifer Burke answered.

81

Jennifer is the youngest child of Gordon Burke, and the younger sister of Jacob.

"Which way did they go?" Kajika asked.

"They went towards Anna's house."

"Thank you Jennifer, you've been a big help."

Kajika turned and looked towards the road to the farms and sighed softly. Just the problem they had feared. That someone would grab one of the small ones to get leverage over the adults.

Just then, Scott arrived with one of the big wagons Peter and Gordon built.

"What happened?" Scott called.

"Gordon's daughter just told me Anna left with a white man in a carriage. It doesn't sound like he got much of a head start on us."

"Jump in!"

Kajika quickly jumped in the wagon and Scott called to his horse:

"Get up Master!" To Kajika he said. "Maybe we can catch up to them."

"It's worth a try." Kajika said.

Kajika sat back in the seat of the wagon and thought. He knew his people were still watching the road by their land. If the carriage tried to out run the wagon; it would be stopped by his people as a precaution.

After closing the blacksmith shop early, Angus MacMillan soon entered the laneway leading to Peter's farm in his own wagon with Josh, Daniel and Sammy. Chance jumped around happily, enjoying the new company. Soon Peter, Sarah and Adam joined them in the barnyard.

"Where's Kajika?" Called Peter.

"Where's Anna?" Sarah cried, her hands clinging to her head in terror.

"The boys noticed Anna was not following them home." Angus started. "Kajika and Scott are looking for her now. Peter, I've already told Sheriff Pollard, and he is getting some men together, and they will be meeting you here.

"I'm going to take Daniel and Sammy back home now; I wanted to tell you about Anna first."

"Thank you Mr. MacMillan." Sarah said. "But will you please take Adam with you? I'm sure Ruth won't mind taking care of him until this is resolved."

"No problem Sarah, I don't think Ruth will mind either. I'm going to stay there for a while, unless you need me back here?"

"I think you could be useful at Ruth's house Sir. Would you please ask Taima if he would join us here? Just in case we need help at the cove? Then Ruth would not be left alone." Peter asked.

"Sure Peter, that's a good idea." Angus replied.

After Sarah put Adam in the bed of the wagon with Sammy, Angus turned his wagon around and headed towards Ruth's farm.

✦

"We're leaving now Jim." The Sheriff told his deputy. "Would you please find out what was the emergency that caused Miss Temple to dismiss school today without notifying any of the parents or the authorities? None of the children should have been left alone early without their parents knowing where they were."

"I'll find out what happened at the school Sheriff." Jim called back to the Sheriff as he watched the posse ride off towards Peter's farm.

✦

"Where are you taking me? Why did you pass my house? You said you wanted to meet with my Poppa?"

Eight-year-old Anna had been crying for a while now. The man had lied to her; he said he wanted her to take him to her house. He said he wanted to meet her father.

When Anna climbed into the carriage, her teacher, Miss. Temple, was in the carriage too, and she wasn't afraid until they passed her farm. The man didn't even slow down when she told him where to turn off the road to the Berry laneway. When Anna started crying Miss Temple

83

called her a crybaby. Miss Temple was so nice in the classroom, why is she so angry now?

"There's a wagon coming up on us now, I thought we could get further away than this." The driver said as he urged his horse to speed up.

"Those children stayed together at the school for a long time before they started to head home." Miss Temple answered him. "Still, whoever was picking them up must have come early."

✦

Shadow noticed the MacMillan wagon before Taima or Ruth, he barked with excitement at the arrival of Angus and the boys. Ruth slowly walked down the stairs and waited by the porch with her hands on her hips. She tilted her head to one side, and tried not to look worried at seeing Adam, and not seeing Kajika.

"What happened?" She said quietly.

"School got out early, and the boys lost track of Anna. Sarah asked if you could watch Adam for a while." Angus told her.

"No problem Mr. MacMillan, Sarah must be beyond worry." Ruth said as she went down the stairs to take Adam from the bed of the wagon.

"Scott and Kajika have gone looking for her. The Sheriff is getting some men together and they will meet Peter at his farm."

Angus turned towards Taima, who had joined them at the wagon. "Taima, I will stay here, Peter asked if you would go to his house now, just in case Sarah needs help."

"No problem Sir. I'll get my horse and leave now." Taima answered.

✦

The scouts protecting the road by the Band noticed a large dust cloud long before seeing the carriage or the wagon. When the vehicles became closer they recognised the wagon chasing the carriage was one of the ones made by the local men. They quickly and carefully positioned themselves to block the carriage at the roadway.

The driver of the approaching carriage steered the horses around the scouts, but they were stopped shortly. Kajika and Scott soon joined them from behind.

"Let us by or I'll hurt the little girl!" A female voice shouted from inside the carriage.

"Why do you want a child?" One of the scouts shouted back as he looked in the carriage and saw Anna.

"We want the Logan boys; their grandfather wants them with him. We will hold this child until you send the boys to us."

Kajika finally noticed who was talking.

"Scott, come here. Look who is behind this."

Scott joined Kajika, and looked in the carriage to see Miss Temple holding a knife at Anna's throat. Poor Anna, her frightened eyes widened to the point where they threatened to jump out of their sockets. Tears streamed down her face.

"Let the child go, we will take you to the Logan farm now." Scott assured Miss Temple.

"I don't believe you." Miss Temple hissed her reply.

"The boys are at the Logan farm, you passed that a long time ago."

"UHHHG!"

"Got her!" Kajika had sneaked to the other side of the carriage and opened the door where Miss Temple leaned as she held Anna.

Anna screamed as Miss Temple fell into Kajika's arms. Scott jumped in the carriage and grabbed Anna from Miss Temple just as Kajika took the knife from her. Anna received a small scratch on her neck, but she quickly lunged into Scott's arms.

"Thank you Uncle Scott! I don't know where they are taking me. I'm sorry I didn't listen to Josh and follow him home."

"Look behind us Anna, look who's coming to bring you home." Scott smiled as he pointed down the road where they could see the Sheriff and his posse heading towards them. Peter was riding in front with the Sheriff.

"Poppa!" Anna wiggled for Scott to let her down from his arms. When she reached the ground, she quickly ran towards her father. Peter jumped down from his horse, and stooped to pick her up in his arms.

By the time the Sheriff reached the carriage, the Scouts had the driver contained. Kajika had contained Miss Temple, moving her back in the carriage.

"So this is the big emergency that caused you to dismiss class early today." Sheriff Pollard stated.

"Thanks again Kajika and all of you brave scouts here. Please thank Siwili and all your people again for me and the whole Town. We are indebted to you forever for all your help today and for all your help over these many years."

When he reached the front of the carriage the Sheriff called: "Scott, Peter, come up here please."

The two men came to the front of the carriage with the Sheriff; Peter still carrying Anna. "Do you remember this one? He's John Daily, Martin's brother-in-law, one of the first men to come here."

Sheriff Pollard had one man from his posse ride the carriage with the two prisoners tied in the back to take them to the jail. Peter checked with the Sheriff to make sure Anna could go straight to her mother. He had Kajika ride his horse back home and rode with Anna in Scott's wagon.

Sarah was having tea with Josh and Taima when Scott's wagon turned into the Berry's laneway. The three jumped from the outside table, but Chance beat them and met the wagon even before it reached the barnyard. When Sarah finally reached the wagon, Anna jumped into her mother's arms crying. The sight of blood from Anna's cut on the neck, frightened Sarah.

"What happened?"

"It was Miss. Temple Momma. I went in the carriage because Miss. Temple said she wanted to see Poppa. She said she didn't know where our farm was."

"Scott, your father brought Adam to Ruth's place because I was in no frame of mind to watch him properly, can you bring him back here for me?"

"Sure Sarah." Scott said, and then he turned the wagon around to head for the Logan farm.

✦

Once settled in the jail, Miss Temple and John Daily were both placed in separate cells, in different rooms so they couldn't communicate with one another.

"Jim," The Sheriff asked his deputy. "How far did you get in your investigation of Miss. Temple?"

"Nowhere boss, no one seems to know anything about her taking time off. Then I asked around to see if anyone knew where she was from, but there was not much information. She had letters from the school board in Chatham, but no one seems to know much about her personal life at all."

"You didn't see us come in here just now, but Miss. Temple was brought in here for abducting the Berry child."

"No! Was it the London people causing trouble again?" Jim asked.

"Yes I think so; Miss. Temple's co-conspirator is none other than our old trouble-maker, John Daily."

Apenimon and five of his men arrived at the Berry farm in time for the evening meal. They found Peter and Josh and Kajika washing up at the well for their upcoming meal.

Apenimon told Peter. "After discussing the problem of Anna's abduction today, we decided you need more help guarding your cove. My men recognized John Daily as the driver. Do you know who the woman calling herself Miss Temple really is?"

"Who is she? Do you know?" Peter asked.

"Not yet, we've sent a messenger to Samuel Patterson asking if he will send his investigator to London to find out. In the meantime, since John Daily was arrested with Miss. Temple I think we have to guard Ruth's farm, and general access to your cove. If they had brought Anna here, they would have seen the cove from your house." Apenimon answered.

"You're right Apenimon. Sarah and I haven't thought much past Anna being here and safe. I'm glad there haven't been any signal lights today." Peter agreed.

"My men and I will stay here tonight to help keep watch and make sure the area is safe. My father is bringing men to Ruth's house too."

"Thanks Apenimon, have you eaten? We have plenty of food, Gordon brought over a deer this afternoon."

"Thanks, we'll join you in shifts. We want someone to be watching all the time." Apenimon then joined his men and they all set off, some towards Berry's cove, and some into the forest.

Siwili and five more men entered the yard at Ruth's home where Scott, Taima and Daniel were washing up for the evening meal. Angus and Sammy were in the kitchen with Ruth.

He repeated the concerns Apenimon expressed to Peter.

"I think you're right too." Scott said. "I'm worried about Peter and his family, living at the cove. Ruth is preparing our evening meal. I'm sure she has enough for you and your men too."

"Thanks Scott. We will join you on shifts; we want to start guarding this area now." Siwili and his men set off, on pre-assigned areas throughout Ruth's property.

In the jail, Sheriff Pollard was getting nowhere with his two new prisoners. Neither one would answer any of his questions, except to say that Martin's father wanted his grandsons with him. Earlier the sheriff had sent a messenger with the paperwork on these two to the circuit Judge. He was hoping for an answer soon.

After the evening meal Scott and Ruth walked hand in hand down near the river. Sammy had gone to sleep, and Daniel and Angus were playing checkers at the kitchen table.

"I'm wondering if this will ever end." Ruth told Scott. "It seems like we have been dealing with Martin's family forever. I feel like this whole problem is because I was taken with Martin and married him."

"I think it's bigger than that Ruth. Your Uncle Samuel's investigators made it plain that David Johnson and his business partners wanted to get a toehold of property in this area. If they hadn't used you, they would have found another way to cause trouble." Scott replied. He put his arm around her shoulder as they continued walking.

"I'm glad you've been here to help over the years. My boys look up to you, as well; you and Peter are such good examples for them to follow.

I'm afraid I'm starting to depend on you." Ruth said as she gently rested her head on his shoulder.

"Now that we know you were never married to him, I am starting to think of you differently. I'm starting to hope you and I can find a way to have a life together."

"I'd like that too."

Suddenly two shotgun blasts rang out in the quiet spring night. Angus' deep voice roared out. "And keep away from here!"

Scott and Ruth ran towards her house and met up with three men from the Band on the way. One of the braves ordered Scott: "You stay with Ruth here until we see what is happening at the farm."

There was a return of blasts, and more yelling.

"My sons — your father" Ruth started.

"We must stay here and let them do what they have to do. They know what they are doing." Scott told her.

Then more shotgun blasts rang out from the Berry farm. Scott led her further in the woods, out of sight of the pathway between the two farms.

As several blasts, yelling and more blasts rang out from both farms, they stood with their arms around one another for strength. They listened to more blasts, running, thumping, groans, and yells. These were mixed with the startled sounds of frightened animals, then horses' breathless snorts and their hooves clumping in the paths. Not soon enough there was quiet. More quiet.

After a while there were timid chirps and clucks of birds and squirrels. Then there were rustles of movement of the small animals around them. Slowly, they too decided to move closer to the path, they looked up and down and saw nothing. Finally they dared to walk into the path and slowly headed towards Ruth's farmhouse.

The scene in the farmyard was chaos. They stood at the end of the yard quietly and took it all in. The light in the kitchen was on and through the window they could see Sammy was up and sitting around the table with Daniel, Scott's father and Siwili. They all looked okay.

The barnyard was full of movement. Someone was being carried to the MacMillan wagon and laid in the bed and three more men, bound by ropes were being led into the wagon also. Several men from the Band were wandering around, picking up guns, and other debris from the yard.

There was running from behind them, and they turned around to see Gordon and his brother, Tim coming towards them.

"What happened here?" Gordon said breathlessly.

"We don't know." Scott said. "Ruth and I were walking down by the river when the shooting started. We missed the action."

"Just as well." Siwili broke in. "I saw you just now from the kitchen. These four tried to storm the house to get your boys but Angus saw them and used your shotgun to ring out the warning shots. We all came here and caught them. I've sent a runner to Peter's farm. We heard shots from there too."

"What about the man they are carrying?" Ruth asked.

I think one of Angus' shotgun blasts hit him. He should be okay." Siwili answered her.

"I know it looks like you have everything under control, but if you need us to help with anything we will stay" Gordon said.

"Thanks Gordon, it looks like we have all the help we need for now. Maybe you should check with Peter." Scott said.

Gordon and Tim left in the direction of Peter's farm.

The scene at Peter's farm was similar to the one at Ruth's. Peter reported to Gordon and Tim that men had tried to storm his farm also. When Sarah saw the two Burke brothers enter the farmyard she called them to the kitchen. The Band members had collected the four perpetrators in one of the wagons Peter and Gordon built.

Peter decided he would accompany two of the Band members to the jail where the Sheriff could add the perpetrators to the two people who were already incarcerated. The men who attacked Ruth's farm would be joining the others. Sarah, Peter, Josh, Gordon and Tim united in prayer around the kitchen table. They thanked the Lord for the safety He provided tonight, and especially for protecting the security at Berry's Cove one more time.

Scott and his father left Ruth and her sons in the company of Siwili and the Band members. The MacMillan men drove their prisoners to Town and met up with Peter and his wagon of prisoners.

"Now I know why I couldn't get any information out of the two I have here." The Sheriff told them. He had gathered some men and met them on the road to Town.

"We heard the gunshots from Town and figured you had some trouble here. I hope I can get some information from these ones."

The Sheriff did get information from the men collected tonight. They were indeed from London. Now the people in London had lost the eight men who had stormed the two farms as well as John Daily and Miss Temple.

Miss Temple turned out to be John Daily's wife. The Sheriff couldn't figure it out. Why were they concentrating on those two farms? Did they know the main landing point was on Peter's farm? Where were they staying while they were in Town? The Sheriff would have heard if that many new people were staying in Town.

More questions than answers.

August, 1846
CHAPTER 6

IN THE COOL OF EARLY MORNING, BATHED IN THE BEGINnings of what promised to be a sun drenched day, a toddler, a young boy and four young men sat along the natural stool at the water's edge of Berry's Cove quietly fishing. It was the first summer after graduation from school for the two now fifteen-year-old friends, and for all the young men, a relaxing beginning for a full day ahead. Adam Berry, now four, Sammy now eight, Daniel, Josh, Taima and Kajika took the time to relax at Berry's Cove before tackling their jobs at the two farms.

Last year, after the attempted kidnapping of Anna and the attempted attack on Ruth's and the Berry's property; Kajika and Taima started helping out for longer times at Peter's farm to add some extra security around the cove.

The residents of Sandwich, and Essex County had weathered the storms of danger and family revelations that happened several years before. Even though the people who threatened Anna and the two farms had spent some time in jail, several men were out now, and the two families remained on guard.

Life goes on and for Daniel and his family; this spring is a new beginning. He was glad his mother and Scott MacMillan finally decided they were in love and were now married, just three months ago. Josh and he had been talking about it for years.

"I can hardly remember my real father any more, and Poppa Scott has been more of a father to me and Sammy. We love him and Poppa Scott's Poppa is good to us too. Now we have a new Poppa and a grandfather too, to love and protect us."

Peter walked his horse slowly down the well-worn road toward the Band property. When Kajika arrived this morning he passed on an urgent message from Siwili and Apenimon for him to meet with them.

Peter decided the news they had to pass on could not be good. At first he wondered why Scott was not invited, because Scott had been active in all the planning since the beginning. Then he remembered the original meeting many years ago, and wondered if it could possibly have anything to do with that subject. It is definitely, not good news.

It is close to eight years since Martin fell off his horse after it stumbled.

At the time, Apenimon described the freak accident: "I was out on evening watch when Martin passed by. He had his horse trotting too fast for the time of night. His horse stumbled and Martin was thrown off. He hit his head on a dead tree trunk which had fallen at the edge of the bush."

Even though Martin was not trusted or even liked in this small community, everyone was worried about Ruth and Daniel.

Samuel had been planning for Martin's eventual departure. Samuel figured Martin would leave Ruth because he would not be getting access to Samuel's property or finances.

The big worry at the time centred around the fact that Martin's accident happened on Band property. There were people in town who would be happy to blame the Band people, or the Negro people. Martin was not pleasant to anyone who did not look like him. It was Samuel's idea to hide his body and pretend Martin just continued on his way as he had done several times before.

Peter knew one of the reasons Samuel gave him the two tracts of land for his own farm earlier was because the cove on that land was sheltered from public access. Samuel had a dream of making the crossing and landings safer for the refugees who came this way.

Peter smiled, Samuel knew him so well, and they shared this dream. Now, after all these years, the dream was realized. Samuel provided most of the finances to get things started, especially for the work on Ruth's farm.

Now many of the refugees stayed in Essex County, and were becoming self-sufficient and helping with the project. Finally, at last all of the labour and most of the food and clothing were donated from local people. It was truly a community project.

Peter was glad Philip was finally transferred out of the Sandwich Post Office this spring. The new person was a young man with his wife; they seemed to be newlyweds from the London area. With all the trouble from London these past years, he was tempted not to trust them. He caught himself, and remembered Sarah's words:

"Not everyone from London can be that way."

"I guess I can at least meet them." He told himself.

✦

The two women, and a young girl now ten, strolled along the path in the woods between their homes, accompanied by two big rambunctious dogs. Ruth, Sarah, and Anna carried wicker baskets to hold the wildflowers they gathered. Shadow and Chance enjoyed running and playing in the woods while staying close to the women. Anna gathered her flowers ahead of her mother and Ruth.

"You know Ruth, Peter and I wondered if you and Scott would ever notice each other!" Sarah laughed.

"Well, Sarah." Ruth mused. "For many years, I didn't consider myself free to think of marrying anyone else. Martin and my failed marriage hung like a cloud over my head. I felt I had ruined my life and my future altogether. Even though it was hard to hear what Martin had done, at least it freed me to love again."

"This Saturday you'll be married three months!" Sarah reminded her. "I'm so happy for you."

"I'm happy too. From the first day we met, Scott has been so good to me. He has always treated me well, and with respect. Scott loves my sons, and has not been afraid to tackle the mess my relationship with Martin caused," Ruth shook her head and continued:

"I don't know how he does it! And Mr. MacMillan loves my sons like they were his own grandsons. Uncle Samuel and Auntie Elizabeth are happy too.

"I've lived alone with my sons for so long now; I had forgotten how to be a wife. Scott is helping me make the change. He is so patient with me and the independent nature I've had to develop over the years!"

Anna ran back to the two women and asked: "Momma are these flowers pretty enough to display in church this week?"

"Yes honey, we will have beautiful flowers for our church and Auntie Ruth's church this Sunday. They can fill our sanctuaries with colours and fragrance provided from our Lord. As long as the flowers are in bloom we can pick them fresh for each Sunday!" Sarah answered her daughter.

She then turned to Ruth and added: "Guess what Ruth! We are talking about building a brick church! The congregation at Sandwich First Baptist are growing to be so many we want to build a more permanent building. Do you know Queen Victoria, herself deeded us the land on Peter Street for our new church building and a graveyard."

"Oh Sarah! That's wonderful! A brick building, and Queen Victoria has granted you the land." Ruth added. "God is blessing this place, and all the people here. Willis Jackson told me he is studying to become a minister for your church. I'm so happy he was married last year, and he and his new wife Cissy now have a little boy. He is really becoming a part of us!"

Sarah laughed. "Yes, Pastor Hubbs thinks he needs some help, with our congregation growing so much! What a blessing! Jackson and Cissy are so happy their little boy Leroy has been born free! Do you know Leroy was named after the old man who taught Jackson how to whittle?"

"Yes, several years ago, Jackson told Scott about how he learned to whittle. Jackson's friend Leroy must have been a wonderful person." Ruth said. She then added: "Sammy is having so much fun since Jackson has been teaching him how to whittle, and he is getting good at it too. Sammy has also started drawing, to help him plan his figures."

"I know! Sammy has given me some of his work!" Sarah laughed.

The women chatted on for a while then separated to deliver the flowers to their respective church sanctuaries before returning home to their families and chores.

◆

"Look at all these fish!" Sammy was laughing! "We'll have to bring some to the Burke's house!"

"Me too, me too!" Chimed in Adam.

"Not this time Adam, we will be going to Sammy's house, not back here." Taima told the toddler, turning to Sammy, he continued:

"Okay Sammy, I'll help you with those fish. Daniel can stay here with Kajika and Josh and help with the fish that stay here. Remember now, we are taking the back way, hidden from the main road."

"I remember Taima."

Sammy remembered well the time he and his mother were taken hostage and tied up in their house. He also remembered the time last year when his old teacher kidnapped Anna in order to get to him and Daniel.

One of the many restrictions put upon Sammy and Anna was that they were not to go anywhere near the main road. They were only to travel along the back way near the river between the three farms of the Berry's, the Logan's (now MacMillan's) and the Burke's. Daniel, Josh and the three younger children were not to travel alone off the property at all. Adults were to accompany them even to school. Adam was not to be off the property at all unless his parents were with him. He was still too young to understand the severe restrictions put on him.

The others, Josh, Adam, Kajika and Daniel went on towards the Berry farm to clean the rest of the fish. Sarah, Anna and Chance met them as they approached the barn to put away the poles and clean the fish.

"We just came from the church!" Anna called to them. "We collected the most beautiful flowers for tomorrow's service!"

"Great job Anna. Momma, where's Poppa?" Josh called back as he lifted the fish higher than Chance could reach to smell. "I want to show him all the fish we caught for today. No Chance! They're not for you!" Josh laughed as he did a little dance to keep Chance away from the fish.

"Poppa had to travel this morning; I'm not sure when he will return." Sarah said quietly.

The women had moved closer to Josh by this time. Sarah did not have a good feeling about the meeting. She didn't understand why the men would have a meeting without Scott.

Scott has been intricately involved with all the planning and security since the beginning. It didn't seem right there should be a meeting without Scott. She didn't even feel free to tell Ruth about the meeting since she felt Scott should be there. This meeting can't be good.

Siwili and Apenimon greeted Peter when he arrived at the Chippewa settlement.

"Greetings dear friend." Siwili said quietly to Peter. "I did not ask Samuel to this meeting since we did something he would not like. I know Scott is Ruth's husband now, but he does not know about our secret."

"True Siwili," Peter answered. "I remember Samuel did not want anyone to know except we who were there at the beginning. I think Scott would understand, but I am not willing to cross Samuel on that point. What did you do?"

"It was me who did something Peter." Apenimon said. "Ever since the people from London started to come looking for Martin, I have been troubled by the package they are talking about. Even though Samuel did not want to look for it, I finely convinced my father to allow me to look in Martin's grave.

"That old cemetery has not been used for many years. Actually; I think Martin is one of the last persons to be buried there. I went with Taima and Kajika two days ago and we uncovered his grave and removed his bedroll and saddlebags. We didn't disturb anything else."

"What was there?" Peter asked. "I've been wondering too."

"The bedroll was just that — but the saddlebags — one side held clothes as we thought, but the other side had two maps and several notebooks. There were notes on everything we were doing here at that time."

Apenimon looked to the ground and shook his head. "Martin was more observant than we thought. I don't know how he gathered all the information. Remember, even Ruth was not told very much at that time because of her relationship with Martin."

Peter nodded, remembering how they worried about what Martin might find out from Ruth at the time.

Apenimon continued. "More importantly, one of the maps he had drawn includes the location of your Berry's Cove and references to it as a prime landing point for the refugees." At the mention of the cove, Peter's breath stopped short.

Apenimon continued his story: "Peter, in Martin's notebook he named all the people who were active at the time, and most of us are active still. You and Sarah, Rev. Hubbs and his family, members of Sandwich Church, Rev. Burke and his sons, Sheriff Pollard, Scott and his father, Seamus and Mary-Ann, Samuel and Elizabeth, and many of their friends from Amherstburg, he even named many of us in the Band, everyone."

Siwili interjected here and added. "We can show you these books now, and you may read them for yourself. I would like to burn them all today, in this fire right after you read them."

He pointed to the small camp fire they had started before Peter arrived. "No wrong person must ever see these notes."

Peter sat silently with his friends by the fire as he read the books and maps. One by one after he read each notebook Siwili placed each in the fire. They all watched the books and maps burn.

When the meeting was done Peter was in no hurry to return home. He walked his horse slowly down the well-worn road towards home. He didn't know how much to tell Sarah. Just what would, or should he do about this new information.

He remembered what Siwili told him before he left the Band.

"Go home for now, Peter. I will see Samuel myself and tell him what we have done. "Stay close to your house, Samuel will probably call a meeting of the original group again soon. Those people from London probably knew what kind of information was in these records, that's why they are so angry and determined."

In his mind, Peter could still see his name and Sarah's on the list, written in Martin's precise handwriting. The image burned in his mind.

If Martin had been able to deliver those documents to London, what would have been the result? What were Martin's plans? To what lengths would he and his cohorts have gone to achieve their goal? Would he and his family even be alive?

He thought about all the other names on that list of Martin's. All good friends he had known these last several years. The people from the Band, Rev Hubbs and many others from Sandwich First Baptist Church, Samuel, Elizabeth, many people he remembered and were still friends from the Amherstburg area, Ruth, both Scott and Angus MacMillan. The list was complete for the time it was written, and it included all people who had become close friends over the years, some even like family.

The only people who were working now on the project not included on the list were the new volunteers. These included mostly people like Jackson, who had come to the Sandwich and Amherstburg area after Martin's death.

When Peter turned into the lane leading to his farmhouse, Josh's voice temporarily broke his solemn mood. "Poppa, you should see all the great fish we caught this morning! Momma saved some for you. We got all our work done, so we can work in the shop. What are your plans today?"

"After I sample your fish, I'll make some decisions." Peter answered quietly. "Is your mother in the house?"

"Poppa, poppa." Cried Adam.

"Yes she is in the house." Josh stopped, and read his father's demeanor. "Is everything okay Poppa?"

"Nothing I can talk about right now," Peter replied as he picked Adam up and gave him a big hug. "I just have to think about all I heard at the meeting this morning." Peter put Adam down when he opened the door to the kitchen, and told Adam to play with Josh.

"Adam, come and help me here in the workshop." Josh clapped his hands and called excitedly to Adam. He could see his father wanted to talk to his mother alone, and wondered what problem was in store for them now.

"Okay Josh." Adam ran to his brother to see what new adventure was in store for him.

Once in the kitchen; Peter took Sarah in his arms, hugged her tight and kissed her deeply. "Oh, my dear heart, I have been keeping something from you for many years. Now we have to talk privately." He sighed, and took a deep breath. "I have been sworn to secrecy, but I have to unburden my soul to you. Please forgive me."

He led her to the bedroom they shared, shut the door, and they sat on their bed. Sarah listened, stunned, as the words he had been holding in all these years spilled aloud. He first told her of Samuel's gift of the farm to them, and Peter's pledge to keep watch over Ruth and Daniel, and later Sammy.

Peter didn't leave anything out when he told Sarah of the events of the night when Martin left home for the last time. He reminded her that his visit the next day was to see about safe passage for the refugees who came the night before. Then he told her Siwili's revelation of the sudden death of Martin. He also told her that Samuel was brought to the old Negro cemetery West of Amherstburg, Martin's burial, and the cover-up of his death.

He even told her it was Martin's horse that was given to the new people who were taken to safety the next day to get it safely out of the area.

Sarah sat listening quietly on the bed beside him. The revelations Peter unfolded to her put many unanswered questions in sharp focus. When he finished talking, she quietly asked him:

"Was there a package with him? Ruth and I have wondered many hours about the package the people from London are always talking about."

"That's what the meeting today was about. The only thing Martin carried with him that night was his bedroll and saddlebags. Finally, this week Apenimon asked his father to allow him to open the grave and search them.

The saddlebags were full, but at the time we thought it was just clothing and we didn't look in them — until this week. Apenimon and Taima, and Kajika went to the cemetery this week to uncover his grave and retrieved the saddlebags. This is why Siwili called me to the Band today. He wanted to tell me what was inside. One side was clothes as we thought, but the other held several notebooks, and two maps of this area.

Martin had been documenting everything we were doing at the time. Somehow he was getting even more information than we were telling Ruth.

Martin knew who had hiding places in their house or barn, and which persons were transporting the refugees out of this area. He knew Gordon and I were building the wagons, and how the Chippewa people were helping us move people to safer places.

Most importantly, the book also listed everyone who was working on the project at that time — everyone, including you and me, the Murphy's, the Burke's the MacMillan's, the Sheriff, of course Pastor Hubbs and the people from Sandwich First Baptist. He even included Ruth, although she wasn't as active then. Seeing our names on that list frightened me, I knew I had to tell you everything after that."

After a deep breath, Sarah said. "This information answers many questions Ruth and I have had over the years. Since the people from London started coming here, we have talked many times about what could have been in the package, and where he could have hidden it. Here he was taking it to his home in London, with all that information about us down here. I wonder what they planned to do with it."

"The worst part is, somehow Martin found his way to our cove. He must have been on our land and searched the shore. There was a map to our cove in his notebook." Peter sighed, "I guess God has been working to keep Berry's Cove a safe place for landings for us even harder than we know."

"Oh my, we can't continue to keep this a secret from Ruth. Did anyone tell Scott?"

"No, at the time they were not together, and Samuel wanted no one to know, other than the people who were at the Band on that day. He hasn't even told Elizabeth or his investigator or his lawyer. Other than me, and now you, no one in Town knows what happened that day."

Peter sighed. "Remember Sarah, it took place on Chippewa land, and Martin was not liked or trusted by many people. Even if we had told what happened at the time, there would be people who would like to blame his death on the Chippewa people, or us."

Now Sarah sighed. "You are right Peter; Martin's death would probably not be seen as an accident by many people. What do we do now?"

After placing the fresh flowers in the sanctuary, Ruth and Shadow headed alone down the stairs of the Sandwich Methodist Church located at the edge of Rev. Burke's property near Sandwich Town. The distance she and Shadow travelled was a little further than Sarah, Anna and Chance had to travel.

"Well Shadow, I wonder if we will be having fish for lunch today."

"Good morning Mrs. MacMillan!" An unfamiliar female voice called to her from the direction of the town.

"Hi." Ruth returned; she didn't recognise the young woman. "Do I know you?"

"No, my husband and I just moved in to town to run the Post Office. I am trying to meet people."

"Oh, I heard there were new people running the Post Office. Do you like it down here in Sandwich Town?"

"We've only been here a week, so I don't know yet. People seem friendly. We met your husband and his father this morning at their shop. He said you would be putting flowers here in the church."

The young woman walked towards her to continue the conversation. Shadow ran up to her and started sniffing around for her to pet him. She recoiled a bit, and then seemed to relax her muscles a little bit.

"Hi boy. What's your dog's name?" She said as she petted him hesitantly.

"His name is Shadow. I wish I had time to talk to you this morning but I have work to do at home. What is your name?"

"It's Shannon Miller, and my husband is Mark. I hope we get to meet you and your family."

"I'll talk to my husband about it. Bye for now." Ruth waved as she called back.

She then went on her way with Shadow.

"Well, Shadow, I hear they're from London," she whispered to him as she petted him. "She must not know much about dogs, she was timid around you. I wonder what the new Postmaster will be like. I hope he and his wife can be trusted more than Philip." Ruth ruffled Shadow's coat around his neck and added. "You're such a good dog Shadow."

When she reached the end of the church's lane, Ruth changed her plans. She and Shadow turned to the main road for home. It was habit for Ruth. The main road was not as secure for her, but with that new woman about she was afraid to be seen using the back path. She did not want to jeopardize the secure route past the farms which followed the river and eventually led to the cove.

A little ways down the road a covered carriage came up from behind Ruth and Shadow and stopped beside her.

"Hello Madame, I wonder if you can show me the way to the Logan farm." He was an older man, about Uncle Samuel's age, well dressed, and with almost white hair. He sat in the passenger seat located inside the carriage. A man, who looked to be in his forties, dressed in a grey uniform and a matching hat with a brim drove the carriage.

"Who are you looking for?" Ruth answered.

"I'm trying to find my son, Martin, but now I'm looking for my two grandsons, Daniel and Samuel Logan." He answered.

Ruth's heart caught in her throat. A new nightmare was upon her. Scott had replaced the sign at the entrance to the farm with: 'MacMillan Farm' a few months ago right after their wedding. She didn't know what to do. She definitely didn't want to lead the man who said he was Martin's father to the home she shared with her sons, and Scott.

Trying to think quickly, she turned around to head back to Sandwich Town. The change in direction confused Shadow, but after she petted him again, she told him: "It will be okay boy." he stayed with her.

Talking to Mr. Logan she said: "I think I will introduce you to our Sheriff, he can arrange a meeting for you with your grandsons."

"I don't want to talk to your Sheriff." He answered gruffly. "I know who you are, and I want to see my grandsons NOW! You have been keeping them from me, and I know you have information about my son too!"

With this angry retort, Shadow started barking and pushing Ruth away from the carriage. Quickly, the driver jumped down and hit Shadow in the head with his handgun. After the initial CRACK of the gun hitting Shadow's head, the silence was deafening. Shadow fell unconscious to the ground.

With an almost simultaneous motion, the driver grabbed a screaming Ruth by the waist and scooped her into the carriage. Suddenly she was face to face with the muzzle of the elder Logan's handgun."

"Quiet woman, don't make a sound." Mr. Logan's voice was low and menacing.

"Has anyone seen Momma?" Daniel called to his brother and Taima.

He had returned home from the Berry's farm with his share of the fish a little while ago, and was getting hungry.

"Not me, can we start lunch without her, I'm hungry." Sammy called back.

"It seems she should be back from the church by now." Taima said. "Let's start lunch and surprise her with the fish we caught."

Taima was quietly worried about the length of time Ruth had taken to come home. It was not like her to stay long without sending word. "I have an idea; let's cook outdoors at a campfire!"

While Taima had the boys cooking at a small fire, he made a larger fire, one with lots of smoke. He sent Sammy to the bunkhouse for an old blanket and showed the boys some 'Smoke Signals'.

"Now I am sending a message to my people that something is not right here. They will start watching the road for strangers." Taima told the boys.

Soon, Angus and Scott came into the yard on horseback from the back path.

"Hi! We closed up the shop for lunch today; we were hoping you caught enough fish for us to share! Did you catch enough?" The two boys stood staring at the men in shock. Taima's concern grew.

"Where's our Momma, Poppa Scott, we thought she might be late because she was visiting you." Sammy asked quietly.

"I saw her and Shadow leave the church a while ago" Scott answered "and I remembered you were all going fishing this morning. Poppa and I decided to surprise you and her. Would she go to visit Mrs. Berry?"

"No" Daniel answered. "She and Auntie Sarah, and Anna were together all morning gathering flowers for the churches tomorrow. She would come straight home for lunch with us."

"What are the smoke signals for Taima?" Scott's face was starting to register the fear that was mounting within all of them.

"I'm just being careful Scott. I want my people to know something's not right here. I decided to cook outside so I could watch this fire. You're right, we have lots of fish."

"I agree Taima it sounds to me like something is very wrong here." Angus interjected.

Angus turned to his son and added: "Don't wait son, you go to Peter's house now and see if he has returned from his meeting. I will go into Town and tell the Sheriff. You lads stay here and watch the fires in case she returns. When I finish with the Sheriff I will return here to do what I can to help."

Scott immediately set his horse towards Peter's farm by the back way. As Angus mounted his horse to leave also, he stopped suddenly when he noticed a slow moving horse being led by Jacob Burke, with Shadow lying over the saddle.

"Help everyone! I found Shadow lying in the road near Town." Jacob called.

Angus dismounted his horse immediately. They all ran to meet Jacob and Shadow. Taima, who arrived first, lifted Shadow from Jacob's horse.

"He's alive." Taima quickly carried Shadow to a clean hay bed in the barn. Everyone followed Taima.

Angus and Taima checked Shadow quickly.

"He's been hit on the head." Angus said, "If Ruth's not with him, she's definitely been taken." He turned to Jacob.

"Jacob, please quickly tell the Sheriff that Mrs. MacMillan's been taken, and ask him to meet us here. Then go directly home and tell your father what happened, we will need him here too."

"Yes Sir." Jacob said, "My mother sent me to the General Store for supplies, while I'm there I will tell Mr. Murphy too before I go home."

✦

Scott entered the back yard of Peter's farm and noticed Kajika, Josh, Anna and Adam looking at the Smoke Signals from Ruth's farm.

"What is happening at the farm Scott?" Kajika asked him.

"Ruth's missing Kajika, is Peter back from his meeting at the Band?"

"Yes, he's in the house with Sarah, they've been there a long time ever since he came home a while ago."

Scott entered the Berry's house from the kitchen door, knocking twice before he walked in, while calling Peter's name.

Peter and Sarah heard him and met him in the kitchen. "Hi Scott, we have to talk to you and Ruth as soon as possible."

"Ruth's missing."

"No! I was hoping they would stop now that Ruth married you." Sarah said. "But they can't, can they Peter."

"We don't have time to tell Scott everything now, Sarah; we have to deal with this new problem."

"Taima has started some smoke signals so his people will know something is going on down here. Kajika was reading them when I came here. I guess we just have to search, and hope they didn't take her far."

Jacob tied his horse to the post by the Sheriff's Office in Town, and ran into the building.

"Sheriff, Mrs. MacMillan is missing, and someone hurt Shadow!" He called as he ran into the office. "I found Shadow on the road as I was coming to Town. When I took him home Daniel and Mr. MacMillan's father told me Auntie Ruth is missing. She didn't come home after leaving Town this morning. She was walking with Shadow."

"Thanks Jacob, can you tell Mr. Murphy while I get my things together?"

"Call Apenimon, there's a fast moving carriage coming from Sandwich Town." A scout from the Band called to one of the other lookouts.

As the first scout left to tell Apenimon, another man noticed Smoke Signals coming from the direction of Sandwich Town.

"Look above, something's wrong in Town we should stop this carriage."

By the time the carriage came upon them, the Band's lookout team surrounded it and quickly stopped the horses. The driver of the carriage pulled out a gun to try to keep the men away from his horses. Two of the scouts jumped up to the seat from their horses, one from each side to overcome the driver.

Quickly two other men from the Band entered the carriage one from each side and overcame Mr. Logan with his gun. There they found Ruth in the back, tied at her wrists and ankles.

"Help! Indians are attacking me!" Mr. Logan yelled out to anyone who would listen.

"Thank you, I was afraid he would take me far away from here." Ruth said to one of her rescuers.

"You — woman; you would be friends with them!" Mr. Logan yelled at Ruth.

"What is happening here?" Apenimon said as he approached the scene from the woods.

"Ruth MacMillan was tied inside the carriage." One of the scouts answered.

"So that's what the Smoke Signals were about. We just noticed them, when I was called here."

As Apenimon helped Ruth out of the carriage, she told him: "This is Martin's father. He was trying to take me to London with him. He and the driver should be brought to the Sheriff in Town. Can you help me Apenimon?"

"Of course Ruth, we will help you back home. They have noticed you're gone, can you see the Smoke Signals?" Ruth looked upwards her eyes following in the direction where Apenimon pointed. There, high in the sky towards her farm, she was relieved to see the message.

"Taima must have sent them up for us. We are answering the Smoke Signals now." Apenimon told her. To the scouts he said.

"I need four men to come with me to help return Ruth home and bring these men to the Sheriff. Also, I need a messenger to ride to Amherstburg to meet my father and tell him and Mr. Patterson what happened here."

Apenimon's men tied Charles Logan and his driver securely and loaded them into the cab of the carriage. Apenimon helped Ruth crawl up to the driver's bench. Once in the seat Ruth's exhaustion overcame her and she collapsed over onto Apenimon. Surprised, Apenimon put his arm around her to hold her in place, and then he quickly turned the horses around toward the farm.

✦

"Let's go to my farm, my father was going to Town to notify the Sheriff. We can coordinate with him there." Scott said to Peter.

"We should all go," Interjected Sarah, "We can help Sammy and Daniel while they wait for news."

"Good," Replied Kajika, "I would like to help too."

At the MacMillan farm, Scott, Peter, and Peter's family found everyone crowded in the barn looking after Shadow, who was still unconscious. Chance, who accompanied his family to the farm, ran ahead emitting a combination whine/howl and reached Shadow first. He sniffed around his brother, continuing in a soft whine. Angus and Taima, who knew the most about animals, had taken the lead in tending to Shadow's needs.

"What happened here?" Questioned Scott,

"Oh Poppa Scott, someone has hit Shadow, and Momma is really gone. Jacob found Shadow on the road from Town, and Momma was with Shadow this morning." Sammy tearfully answered.

"I sent Jacob to Town for the Sheriff, son, I didn't want to leave Shadow. It will take both me and Taima to take care of him. It looks like he will at least lose the use of his left eye."

"Someone just left Shadow in the road?" Scott said blankly.

Peter broke in the conversation. "We have to start looking for Ruth, if Shadow was found on the road out front; it makes sense that whoever took her must be travelling on the same road. It's a good thing the people from the Band are getting word through the Smoke Signals Taima sent."

"Look up here now, our people have seen the signals and are returning the message." Kajika exclaimed from outside the barn where he had been keeping an eye on the sky.

"I will let them know we have seen their message now." Kajika then ran to the fire, which had been neglected since Shadow was brought home.

Just then the Sheriff came down the lane with Seamus and Jackson. Jackson had been placing some of his carvings at Seamus' store to be sold when Jacob came with the news of the attack on Shadow, and Ruth being missing.

"Scott, you stay here with the boys and Shadow. Peter, can you join us for a search down the road?" The Sheriff said to the men.

The truth was Scott was in shock. With Shadow being hurt so badly and Ruth missing; his normally quick mind was cloudy.

Angus and Taima concentrated on helping Shadow. Kajika was tending the signal fire and helping Sarah with Anna and Adam. The older boys, who would not leave Shadow's side, sat with Scott and Chance. They all sat together, near those working on Shadow. Scott rested his head lightly on Chance's shoulder, speaking softly and petting him. He turned his head slightly and stared blankly at Shadow, and then he wondered what would happen next.

The Sheriff, Peter, Seamus, and Jackson, left down the lane from the MacMillan farm; and were joined by Gordon, and his brother, Tim at the main road.

"I was working with Gord on a building project when Jacob came with the news. I hope I can help too." Tim said.

"We need all the help we can get Tim. I'd like to split up, because we're not sure where they have taken Ruth. Peter and Tim, come with me towards the Band property, and Seamus, Jackson and Gord, will you go through Town and then head towards Windsor? Don't go far past Windsor; they seem to do most of their travelling along the west end of the County. I'm thinking we might get to them. Stop people in Sandwich and Windsor and ask if they have seen any strangers on the road."

"Sure Sheriff, we'll keep our eyes out for anything unusual." Seamus answered.

✦

The Sheriff's group had gone about a mile down the road, almost to Pastor Hubbs farm when they met Mr. Logan's carriage. It was accompanied by several members of the Chippewa Band and driven by Apenimon with Ruth by his side. Ruth had by that time somewhat recovered from her collapse.

"Is that Apenimon driving that carriage and Ruth beside him?" Said the Sheriff.

"It is! I'm going back to get our other team now!" Tim exclaimed as he turned his horse around to catch up and stop the team of men going towards Windsor.

"What a wonderful sight! Thank you Apenimon, we were just getting our search under way for Ruth." The Sheriff called to them.

"We saw the Smoke Signals from here and then noticed the carriage coming fast past our land. Something's wrong with Ruth, she fainted after we helped her in the passenger seat up here." Apenimon answered.

"I just want to go home and see if everyone is okay," Ruth said, slowly and still shaken up from her ordeal.

"Mr. Logan's driver hit Shadow hard on the head with his gun before he grabbed me. Is Shadow okay?"

"Jacob Burke found Shadow on the road where he was left and took him home. Now Mr. MacMillan and Taima have Shadow resting in your barn, and are seeing to him. He's not good. When we left them, he was still not conscious." Peter answered.

"Wait a minute, what were you saying Ruth? Mr. Logan is here?" The Sheriff asked her.

"Yes Sheriff." Apenimon answered for Ruth. "Inside the carriage we have Martin's father and his driver. The driver hit Shadow and grabbed Ruth and put her in the carriage. When we rescued her she was tied up inside the carriage with Mr. Logan holding a gun on her."

"Sheriff," Peter said. "Ruth still looks shaken up; can we take the carriage to her farm, rather than have her sit on a horse to go home?" Peter said.

"Sure Peter, Apenimon, can you and your men help us as far as the jail? I will also need a statement from all of you."

"Of course Sheriff."

"Finally!" Mr. Logan hollered from inside the carriage. "I see some White people! What is all this talking about? This woman has been keeping my grandsons away from me, and hiding my son. I don't know where he is. It is all her fault, she must have driven him away or had him captured somewhere. What about me and my problems?"

"Quiet! You kidnapped her! We will see to you and your problems when we get you to the jail." The Sheriff hollered back at him.

✦

When the party arrived at the farm and turned down the lane, Sarah and the children reached the carriage first and greeted the travelling party with shouts of joy and relief!

Slowly, almost afraid to know what had happened, Scott left Chance alone to sit at Shadow's side so he could see how Ruth was doing.

Scott helped Ruth down from the passenger seat of the carriage and held her close before he let her stand on her own.

"How are you? Did they hurt you?" He whispered softly.

"No, I was just afraid I would not be rescued in time. How is Shadow?" Ruth answered him. "Shadow was trying to push me away from the carriage, but the driver jumped down and hit him, then grabbed me." She added.

From inside the carriage Charles Logan hollered. "Are these my grandchildren? What are these Indians and Negros doing here? What kind of a place is this?"

At once one of the scouts from the Band jumped in the carriage and held Charles Logan's own gun on him and quietly said:

"You be quiet, didn't you hear? Your grandchildren are worried about their mother, and their dog, and you are responsible for all of this."

Mr. Logan's driver hissed from beside him: "He's right, we're in enough trouble right now. Be quiet and don't add to our problems."

Everyone in the yard stopped talking and looked toward the carriage. After the scout jumped in the carriage, and the yelling stopped; they resumed their original conversations. The Chippewa scout stayed in the carriage until it was time to leave the farm to make sure Mr. Logan stayed quiet.

"My Poppa and Taima are seeing to him, he is still not conscious. They both think if he lives he will lose his sight in his left eye. They just don't know much yet."

"Ruth, you rest up here, remember, you fainted before." Apenimon said more for the benefit of Sarah and Scott than for Ruth.

"You fainted! My dear, you must come with me in the house and let the others take care of Shadow and everything else going on around here."

Sarah took charge of Ruth. From behind she placed her two hands on Ruth's two shoulders and guided her into the house. She even turned to wave Scott away from them.

"I'll make us some tea and a light meal. You sit on the chesterfield and put your feet up and rest after this horrible ordeal. Anna, come and help me."

Anna, recognizing the tone in her mother's voice quietly followed her mother and Ruth. She quickly looked behind a couple of times, but she knew there was no choice but to follow her mother's lead immediately.

Outside, Scott stood alone in the yard. First he watched Sarah lead Ruth into the house with Anna following. Slowly, he turned to see what was going on around him. He stopped and watched the Sheriff, his men and the Chippewa party. The scout who quieted Mr. Logan had left the carriage and was back on his own horse. They rode the carriage down the lane and turned towards Town.

Next Scott turned towards the barn and watched his father and Taima return to the barn with Daniel, and Josh who held Adam by the hand to be with Shadow and Chance. He turned again to see Kajika and Sammy return to the fire, to make sure the message to the Band had been read.

Still in shock he then turned back towards the house, wondering if he should have let Sarah take charge of Ruth. He stopped again, and then started walking towards the barn to see how Shadow was doing. It was then when Peter took his shoulder and gently turned Scott towards the bunkhouse.

"Meet me in the bunkhouse," Peter put his arm around Scott's shoulder and said softly.

"I'm going to get you something to eat and bring it in there. Ruth is safe with Sarah. The Sheriff will come here to take any statements he needs. People are taking care of the children and Shadow. You and I need a meeting and you have to listen carefully to everything I have to say to you now."

Peter met Sarah in the kitchen, neither Scott nor Ruth had eaten, nor Peter for that matter. They all would need a decent meal to continue the day ahead.

"After Scott and I have something to eat I'm going to talk to him now, he has to know." Peter told her.

"Anna is helping Ruth get settled in the living room right now. I don't know about Ruth." Sarah said. "If she has fainted, I want to see how she is doing before I talk to her. You go ahead and talk to Scott. They both shouldn't be in the dark any longer about what is really going on."

Shortly, Peter joined Scott in the bunkhouse with the food he promised. While they both ate Peter took a deep breath, and started his story for the second time today.

"Those Indians just rode up and attacked my carriage for no reason." Mr. Logan kept repeating. "We weren't doing anything except riding down the road. No one down here seems to care my son is missing and has been for many years. That woman knows something about it and she's keeping me from seeing my grandsons. MY GRANDSONS! I have a right to see my grandsons."

"We told your men years ago, your son left this town and the woman who he pretended to marry. Ruth was with child at the time and he left his older son. I don't see you looking anywhere else for him.

"All I see you doing is searching her property for this mysterious package you think he left here, and tormenting your grandsons and Ruth. I don't see you are very worried about your son at all.

"You went too far this time. You kidnapped her, tied her up and held her at gunpoint. Your driver attacked her dog, your grandsons' pet and protection. That doesn't sound like someone who is worried about anyone but himself." The Sheriff hollered angrily back at him.

The Sheriff slammed the iron bar door of the jail cell behind the two men and locked it.

After the sheriff left the cell area, the driver hissed at Charles Logan again:

"Look what you've involved me in! This is kidnapping! You said you wanted to visit your granddaughter and her new husband. Who is that woman you had me take for you and all the other people down here who interest you. What were you talking about when you said that woman had your grandsons?"

"You be quiet and do what you're told. I hired you to keep me safe as well as being my driver." Charles said. "I don't want that Sheriff hearing any conversations we have between us."

"You old fool; I didn't come down here to get arrested!" The driver retorted.

When he reached his office, Sheriff Pollard started the interviews with Apenimon and carefully recorded the statements from him and his men in his notebook. He also had Apenimon relate what Ruth told him while they were riding back to the farm in the carriage. The story was starting to come together. The Sheriff still didn't understand why all of a sudden, after a year with no word or threats at all Martin's father came down to Sandwich Town himself. Every time they tried something before he had just sent employees. Also, just what had him interested all over again?

In the barn Angus and Taima had to face the fact Shadow was not going to recover from the injury of his attack. They looked, knowingly at each other, and the sad, unspoken message passed between them. Angus slowly got to his feet, moved closer to the door and called the boys over to him.

"Shadow's not getting any better boys; it's just a matter of time now. We're going to have to face the fact Shadow's time has come. You should decide if he had a favorite blanket to wrap him in and where you want to bury him."

Daniel, Sammy, Josh and Adam's eyes silently started to tear up as the kindly old man talked. Chance couldn't be moved from his brother's side, and no one had the heart to try at this point. Taima moved closer to Chance, and took over where Scott had left off, comforting the Berry's dog. Adam tearfully crawled in Taima's lap.

In the house, Ruth sat in the living room, on the chesterfield, with her feet elevated on an ottoman. Anna brought Ruth a tray of food and Sarah carried a tray holding a pot of tea, three cups and saucers and placed them on the coffee table.

Sarah sat beside Ruth on the chesterfield, and Anna took her place in a nearby armchair. While Ruth related the story of her capture, Sarah gauged how Ruth was physically and mentally.

"You look pale, my friend, are you sure you don't need to rest?"

"I'm worried about Shadow. Anna dear, can you go outside to the barn and see if there's any change in his condition?" As Anna, eager for the chance to run outside to check on Shadow left, Ruth smiled and answered Sarah's question.

"My dear friend Sarah, I can't hide anything from you can I? I'm with child, not very far along. I haven't even told Scott, but I think he might suspect."

"Maybe you should go to bed. You don't want to risk losing the child." Sarah worried.

"I think if I just stay here with my feet up, I'll be okay. I'm going to stay home for a few days too. Scott, Daniel and Sammy can help with the cooking and heavy things for a while."

"Sure, you just stay here. By the way, Peter has taken Scott to the bunkhouse. Neither he nor Scott has eaten, so Peter brought some food for them too. They are talking in there."

When Anna had almost reached the barn, Chance started to howl. She ran to the barn and was met shortly by Peter and Scott running from the bunkhouse.

Inside the house Sarah and Ruth looked at each other then hung their heads, they knew what had happened in the barn.

Shortly after the small mourning party finished the grave, all the children gathered around the perimeter for prayers, and they decorated it with flowers. Later, Peter took notes for a suitable wooden marker, as dictated by the children. The marker he would make later.

Taima and Kajika were hesitant to leave after the long day. There was still no word from the Sheriff or any of the Band members who went to Town with him. They stood outside the barn talking to Angus and Scott MacMillan.

Soon a familiar buggy came down the lane carrying Uncle Samuel and Aunt Elizabeth. They were accompanied by Siwili and the three members from his Band who had been sent to Amherstburg to notify him and the Patterson's of the goings on here.

"Siwili was visiting me, and this small party came and told us what happened here today. What is going on over there?" He pointed to Peter and the children standing by Shadow's grave.

"Who did you bury? Where is Ruth?" Uncle Samuel was stricken.

"Ruth is okay, she is resting in the house, and Sarah is with her. We buried Shadow. He was very brave and tried to save her from being captured." Scott answered.

"Oh no, I'm so sorry about Shadow, but I must go in the house to see Ruth." Aunt Elizabeth exclaimed, as Angus helped her climb down from the buggy. First she ran to the grave to hug Daniel and Sammy and then headed towards the kitchen door.

When Sammy saw his uncle, he ran to him with Daniel right behind.

"Uncle Samuel, Shadow was so brave, he tried to push our Momma away from the bad man, and the bad man hit Shadow on the head with his gun." Sammy sobbed to Uncle Samuel.

Daniel was sobbing too and said. "Taima and Grandfather MacMillan tried to make him better, but they couldn't save him."

"Yes." Added Sammy. "Shadow is such a brave dog!"

"The beautiful dog was a fighter, but the blow to his head was too deep. His left eye was mangled too. I guess there was just too much damage." Angus sadly stated.

While the boys led Siwili, Uncle Samuel and the party over to Shadow's grave, Adam ran to Uncle Samuel with his hands raised to be picked up. Uncle Samuel obliged Adam and included a big hug.

"I see Chance is on guard." Uncle Samuel noticed, as he gave Adam and extra hug. "The two dogs are very close. Chance will need a new friend soon. That's a beautiful tribute boys." Uncle Samuel said solemnly regarding Shadow's grave and Chance's demeanor.

"Samuel, we were wondering what was going on down in Town." Peter said. "We haven't heard anything since Apenimon, his men, and the Sheriff left for Town with the kidnappers. Did you know that it was Mr. Logan himself, Martin's father who came down this time and it was him who was holding Ruth at gunpoint?"

"Gunpoint! No! I would like to have a talk with THAT man." Samuel said.

"Anna." Peter called his daughter over to them. "How is Auntie Ruth feeling?"

115

"She's just resting Poppa. Momma has her feet propped up on the ottoman and they were just talking when they sent me out to see about Shadow. I went back in and told them when he passed, but Auntie Ruth just wanted to stay in the house and rest."

"Scott, will you stay and watch things here? I would like to go with Samuel into town and see what is going at the jail."

"We will go on to Town with you Samuel," Siwili added.

"Sure Peter, I don't want to go far from Ruth and the boys now." Scott returned. "By the way, ask about that new couple who are running the Post Office. They were in our shop this morning asking too many questions about Ruth and the boys."

"I was wondering about them too, but Sarah said I should give them the benefit of the doubt." Peter answered.

"After today, I'm afraid I have to be convinced to give anyone the benefit of the doubt." Scott said.

"I agree with you there Scott." Samuel said, "Can you tell Elizabeth, Ruth and Sarah where Peter and I have gone?"

"No problem, the women have had possession of my wife long enough. I think it's time I go in the house to see for myself how she is doing." Scott answered with a smile.

Scott turned to his father; "I won't be coming back to the shop today. Did we leave anything which must be taken care of before the day is out? I don't remember."

"No son, we left everything safe, and nothing has to be done today. I'll be staying here for a while yet, to make sure the children are doing okay. You go in the house and see your wife. I'll not leave before telling you." Angus told his son.

"Thank you Poppa," Scott answered his father. "Shadow was a great loss. I'm glad Ruth seems to be okay." Slowly, Scott headed for the kitchen door.

After first hearing the news Peter relayed to him, he didn't know how to put things together. Now after thinking about it, many of the unanswered questions about what had been going on all these years were coming together.

Peter said Sarah would be telling Ruth, if she thought she was up to it. He wondered if Ruth knew yet, and how she took the news. She was devastated after the revelation about Martin's other family and his real reasons for coming to Amherstburg. What could be going on in her mind now?

When Scott entered the kitchen he could hear Aunt Elizabeth and Sarah fussing over Ruth in the Living Room.

"Oh my goodness! Is a man allowed in this room?" Scott laughed as he peeked in the living room. "May I please see my wife?"

"Of course, Scott, we are just trying to keep her quiet and calm. Is there any word from Town about Mr. Logan and his driver?" Sarah asked.

"No Sarah, but Peter and Uncle Samuel asked me to let you ladies know they are going there now to check on what is happening."

"Good" Aunt Elizabeth said. "I don't know why those people from London are still looking here for Martin, after all these years. They should start looking somewhere else." Scott immediately realized Uncle Samuel still hadn't told Aunt Elizabeth about the secret the men have been keeping all these years and today's revelations. He exchanged looks with Sarah, and realized he had better be careful about what he said.

Sarah smiled and said: "Come in the kitchen Auntie Elizabeth, we should start an evening meal for everyone and leave Scott and Ruth alone to talk."

After the women left, Scott said: "How are you darling? Do you have everything you need?" Scott sat down beside Ruth on the chesterfield and took her hands in his.

"I have everything I need now Scott, and a big surprise for you!" Ruth smiled.

◆

"Grandfather's carriage is still by the jail. I should go over and see if he is well." Shannon told her husband of just one month.

"Be still Shannon, if you let on we are related to him, we will lose this position at the Post Office for sure. Then will be no information coming from here to London at all again." Mark told her.

"I know your right, but he's my Grandfather, and I haven't seen my brothers yet either. Still no one has found my father. Mother is afraid he's been murdered."

"Be patient Shannon, your Uncle John, and my Uncle Herbert saw them bring your Grandfather and his driver in. I saw Uncle John leave to tell our people in London. Someone should be here tomorrow; my uncle is a lawyer and will go over to the Sheriff's office to see what can be done now. We just have to wait and see what happens."

"Who are those people that just arrived? That old man has a Negro and some more Indians with him! What a place!" Shannon exclaimed as

Samuel's carriage Peter, Siwili and those accompanying them drove up to the Sheriff's Office.

※

"Hi Sheriff," Peter said as he, Siwili and Uncle Samuel followed him into the office. The rest of the men stayed outdoors to visit with those who had already given their statements to the Sheriff. "We were wondering how the investigation is coming along. Is there anything we can do to help?"

The three men entered the office which was occupied by some people from the Band who were finishing up with their statements. As each man finished his statement; he went outdoors to join the growing group near the stairs.

"How are Ruth and Shadow?" The sheriff asked. Everyone in the room waited for the answer.

"Ruth is resting and a bit shaken up, but she seems unharmed. Samuel said. "Shadow passed away a little while ago. Ruth told us he tried to push her out of the driver's way to save her. The children were burying him when I arrived." The flat tone in Uncle Samuel's voice told his sorrow over the attack on his niece and the loss of the family dog.

"Shadow was a good dog. I'm sorry about him, but I'm glad to hear Ruth is well." Apenimon added.

"I agree, Shadow was a good dog, I'm sorry about him." The Sheriff replied. "I'll go out to the farm to get statements from Ruth and Scott tomorrow. I don't want to bother them today. When you came to Town did you see the deputy I sent out to the road where Ruth was taken to try to find some clues?"

"I saw him," Peter replied. "I wondered what he was doing. I hope he finds something that can help."

"Charles Logan isn't saying anything except Ruth has been keeping him from his son, and from seeing his grandsons. The driver is another story; he is angry and talking up a storm. He asked me to get him away from Logan.

"Once he was able to talk to me in private, he told me Charles hired him to take him to see his granddaughter and her new husband. By the way, they are the new Postmaster and his wife. He said he wasn't told anything about another family or that kidnapping was involved and is willing to help in the investigation."

"Granddaughter!" Peter, Siwili and Samuel looked at each other as they answered together.

"And her new husband." Added Peter, "Oh no, I was afraid the new Postmaster and his wife were a replacement for Philip. Scott told me they were in the Blacksmith shop this morning asking too many questions about Ruth and her sons."

"Peter." The Sheriff asked slowly. "Who is helping Scott and Ruth at the two farms now? If what you are saying is true, Mark and Shannon Miller must know their job is not secure and will try to cause trouble there." The Sheriff asked him.

"Those two must be the reason for the sudden interest again." Added Siwili. "I need some men to go to both farms and secure the properties. And just as important, he added, make sure Berry's Cove stays secure." He said turning towards his son.

Apenimon said. "I will gather some of our men waiting outside and take care of it now, Father."

✦

"A baby! No wonder you were overcome after the kidnapping! We have to take especially good care of you now!"

Scott was ecstatic, and also worried. With the trouble starting up again, he wanted to keep Ruth out of the line of fire.

"I was thinking." Ruth added. "Now that the trouble seems to be starting up again, we should all move in with your father for a while for more security.

"Do you think we could let the farm out to someone who can be trusted, who needs a place and will take care of it? They would have to understand the extra responsibilities around the activity at the cove until we can move back. I want to be able to rest more now, until the baby is born."

"We are both thinking the same thing Sweetheart." Scott smiled. "My father and I will work out the details, but you and I have to talk about something else which has happened today before you were taken."

Ruth now heard third-hand what Apenimon told Peter, and Peter told both Sarah and Scott that morning. She sat quietly throughout the telling of the story, but as his narrative continued, Scott could see signs of anger rise in her face. He couldn't tell who would be taking the brunt of her anger.

At the end, before she was able to respond, there was a quiet knocking at the door, and Angus MacMillan entered.

"Hi my son, and his beautiful wife, Apenimon and his party are coming down the lane; I thought you might like to know. The ladies who were in the kitchen have gone out to meet them."

"Papa, Ruth has just told me wonderful news; you will be a Grandfather soon!" Scott beamed.

"Oh!" Angus threw up his strong arms and then clutched his face in surprise. "Thank you! Thank you my children, what a wonderful news addition to this sad day." Angus exclaimed.

He leaped over to Scott and Ruth, and as gently as an old blacksmith is able, and enveloped both in a big bear hug.

"We should spread this wonderful news right away."

"Please no, Papa, I am not very far along. Ruth begged. "After the excitement today, I would like to stay quiet for a while."

"Of course dear heart, whatever you say, but do your Auntie and Uncle know?"

"No, not yet, we are telling you now because we have a big favour to ask." Ruth replied.

"Yes, Papa, you and I will have to plan soon; I'm concerned about safety for Ruth and the boys, with this trouble starting up again." Scott added.

"May we make temporary arrangements to move in with you? We will have to find someone to live here who can be trusted to carry out the task of helping the refugees who are still steadily arriving. I want to keep Ruth and our sons out of the line of fire."

After a couple of knocks on the door, they heard a soft: "Hello." Apenimon solemnly entered the living room where Scott, Ruth and Angus were talking.

"I have disturbing news from Town. The Sheriff said the new Postmaster's wife is Charles Logan's granddaughter. He think's Ruth and the boys should be moved in Town or to Samuel's place where they can be better protected."

"Oh—now I know," Ruth said slowly. "This morning she said her name was Shannon, and I couldn't figure out why her name bothered me. Martin's oldest child from London, her name is Shannon. Uncle Samuel's investigator told us when we found out he was married before he came here. There was Shannon, Gabriel, and Jeanne. Those names are burned into my memory."

"I knew there was something wrong when they were asking all those questions about you and the boys." Scott said.

"Aye Laddie, me too, I was uneasy with all those questions about you and how they wanted to socialize with the family. They just moved into Town, and the way they targeted Ruth and her boys didn't sit well with me." Angus added.

"I have come here with our men from this morning;" Apenimon added. "We think you should have some extra security around here and the Berry farm, especially the cove, until this new trouble has been handled. One of my men saw John Daily head off while we were bringing Charles and his driver in with the carriage. I'm sure they will have reinforcements here by tomorrow."

"John Daily, is he out of jail already? I'm sure you're correct about the reinforcements by tomorrow Apenimon." Angus agreed.

There were no customers in the Post Office and Shannon stood a little back from the large window so she couldn't be seen.

"We haven't seen Ruth, her new husband or that old blacksmith or my brothers come in or out of the Sheriff's office yet." Shannon said. "I wonder what happened when grandfather went to the farm."

"I thought your grandfather was just going to visit and try to see your brothers, am I right?" Mark asked.

"That's what he said; maybe they gave him some trouble." She answered. "Were you able to find directions to the farm yet?"

"No. No one will tell me anything about where they live, or about the activities around the slaves they bring over. I know something big is going on around here. I think your grandfather came down here too soon, we haven't had a chance to make friends yet."

"I can't stand just waiting." Shannon said, but she mirrored both their feelings.

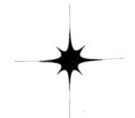

Apenimon, Kajika and Taima decided to join one of the scouts from earlier and go down to the cove and check there. There had been no one at the Berry home all day because of the trouble at the MacMillan farm. If someone had risked a daylight crossing they wanted to be there to help. Three men had gone to the Berry home and two others stayed at the MacMillan home.

The cove was quiet, but there was a signal light from the other side of the river. The men looked up to the Berry house behind them on the rising and saw their men had seen and were answering the signal. Shortly, the response signal came, there would be five people coming by rowboat tonight.

"I am going over to see Sarah at the MacMillan's now. You men patrol this area, check if there are signs that anyone has been here while we were occupied at the MacMillan farm. I will send someone from there to the Band; we will need more people here for tonight." Apenimon told the others.

"Sure." Said Taima. "When you send word to the Band, ask for Amitola and a few other women to come and help Ruth and Sarah. Ruth really appreciated Amitola's help before. Ruth said the company helps her to keep calm."

Kajika and Taima waved to the men at the Berry house to signal they got the message and pointed to Apenimon as he left for his errand.

"Good idea, I'll remember that." Apenimon called as he went on his errand.

The men up at the house were now able to concentrate on checking the house and surrounding areas to make sure things were secure for tonight.

At the MacMillan home, Scott called Daniel and Sammy into the house to quietly tell them the news of the new baby.

"Now listen carefully to me boys," Ruth told them. "I'm not very far along and after the fright today, I have to stay quiet and calm. I might still lose the baby, and I don't want to tell everyone about it yet."

"Also, sons, in order to help your mother stay calm, we are going to move temporarily to our house behind the Blacksmith shop. As well, I am going to hire someone to help with your mother's work." Scott added.

"Will you be okay Momma?" Sammy asked. "I really would like to have a new brother or sister."

"I am glad for the new baby, but I'm worried too Momma. Do Uncle Samuel and Auntie Elizabeth know yet?" Daniel asked.

"Not yet son, we will tell them at the evening meal when we are all together." Ruth said. "Please don't talk about it to anyone, including Josh and Anna until we are able to tell your Auntie and Uncle!"

"Okay Momma and Papa Scott." Said Daniel. "Oh! Here comes Apenimon from the back trail really fast!"

Scott left Ruth on the chesterfield and rushed for the door with Angus to meet Apenimon.

"What's happening at the Berry's house?"

"Our friends were signalling from Detroit when we arrived. There will be five people coming over tonight. I'm going to Town to tell Peter, and send some men to our Band for more help. We will be asking two or three women, including my sister to help Ruth and Sarah." Apenimon told the men quickly. He then hurried off towards Town.

Sarah and Elizabeth were talking with the two men from the Band who were left to help at the farm and noticed Apenimon pass through quickly. They joined Scott and Angus and were told the new information.

Sarah said once the meal was prepared; she and Anna would be going home and start preparing there for the people who would be coming tonight. She said she would also be taking Josh and Adam. The two men from the Band decided to check the surrounding wood and the paths near the water.

Daniel, who had also come out from the house and overheard the exchange, asked Josh to help him make up the beds and prepare linens and other supplies in the bunkhouse for tonight until he went home to help his mother.

"I'm glad we are old enough to help out now, soon Sammy will be able to help too." He told Josh.

"Yes, Anna is helping as much as she able already." Josh answered.

✦

Two pair of eyes watched Apenimon as he rushed up to the Sheriff's office. "Something's going on in that direction." Shannon said. "Now that your uncle, our new lawyer has finely gone in the office he can help my grandfather and then tell us what is going on. I'm going out for some fresh air and to see where the activity is."

"Be careful not to trespass onto private property, we don't want to make more trouble than we might be facing already. Whatever happened must be serious; this activity has gone on too long." Her husband answered.

When he arrived at the Sheriff's Office Apenimon stopped at the outer door where some of the Band members were talking and waiting for Siwili.

Quietly, in the Chippewa language so there would be less chance of being overheard, Apenimon said: "I need two men to go back to the Band now and organize some help for tonight.

"Ask my sister to bring friends to come and help the women here with the cooking and prepare for five people who are landing at the cove tonight. Ruth is still overcome, and Sarah needs help."

"We'll go now." Two men quickly offered.

Once inside, Apenimon saw a stranger in the office. He touched Peter quietly on the shoulder and said: "Peter, I need you outside now." When they were safely away from the building he told Peter what was going on at his home.

"I'll leave now Apenimon, but we need you as an eyewitness inside, Charles Logan must have travelled with his lawyer, and he is here now trying to get him out on bail. We definitely can't risk people wandering around the area with new refugees coming here tonight."

"Also, Peter," Apenimon added. "Ruth thinks the wife of the new Postmaster might be Martin Logan's daughter by his marriage in London. We're going to have to keep a close eye on those two."

"Oh no." Mumbled Peter as he ran down the steps of the building, mounted his horse, and left.

Once inside the office again, Apenimon looked around to get his bearings.

The Sheriff quickly noticed him and asked him over to his desk.

"Apenimon, this is Mr. Logan's lawyer. He says you and your men attacked Mr. Logan's carriage without provocation."

Apenimon considered the well-dressed stranger from out of town with his 'puffed out' chest and superior air about him.

"We had a signal from the MacMillan farm that something was wrong there; when we saw the carriage racing down the road by our land, we thought it might have something to do with the trouble at the farm. Please tell me Mr. — lawyer sir, what reason did Mr. Logan give you for kidnapping Mrs. MacMillan and having his driver kill her dog in the process?"

"How dare you speak to me in that tone of voice?" The lawyer hissed at Apenimon, then turned to the Sheriff: "What kind of a Sheriff are you that you would take the word of an Indian over me?"

"Actually Mr." He checked the business card the lawyer provided him earlier. "Russell, I'm the kind of Sheriff, who saw how upset Mrs. MacMillan was after the fact, and saw the guns and the rope in the

Under The North Star

carriage. I also saw the blood at the side of the road where her dog was left to die and I heard Mrs. MacMillan's side of today's story.

"Furthermore, I've been living here and have seen all the previous attempts to harm her and her sons by Mr. Logan's people. We have prosecuted his people before, and will do so again. Just who does your client think he is to come down here and try to bully the people in this Town?" The Sheriff's anger towards Mr. Logan, and distain for the lawyer Mr. Herbert Russell who would represent him, was hard to contain.

Flustered by the anger and the facts the Sheriff spouted Mr. Russell quietly replied: "My client is really just trying to find out what happened to his son so many years ago."

Still angry, the Sheriff said: "We told him. Martin Logan left town leaving the woman he pretended to marry with a seven year old son and with another child on the way. He was angry and said he would never return. Frankly, he didn't get along with many people here, and many were not sad to see him go.

"Your client talks about looking for his son, but he has sent people here to look for some papers he said his son was planning to bring to him. We don't know about any papers, and we have looked ourselves.

"He even had Mrs. MacMillan and one of her sons held captive in her own house at gunpoint. They were tied to chairs in the kitchen while his men searched her whole house for the papers. Those men weren't looking for his son that day. I led the posse who rescued her and her son.

"Your client will stay here in jail and wait until the judge comes, and then he will stand trial. We have lots of evidence and witnesses for his activities today."

"I'll be back." Herbert Russell quietly left the Sheriff's office.

✦

Mr. Russell stormed into the Post Office and immediately stopped short and contained his temper. There was one customer in the Post Office; Mark Miller looked up from servicing his customer and immediately went back to his task at hand.

Mr. Russell moved over and stood at one of the writing desks near the large front window and busied himself by going through the papers in his briefcase. The customer, a storekeeper from Windsor was sending several parcels, taking his time and asking questions. Mr. Russell pulled out some papers and started writing a quick letter… The letter grew longer… Mr. Russell shifted his feet and position several times while lengthening his letter. Finally the customer thanked Mark for his service and left. As soon as the customer shut the door after himself Mark spoke.

"What happened today with Shannon's Grandfather?"

"Where is Shannon?" Mr. Russell angrily answered Mark.

"She couldn't contain herself here any longer. She went out to see what was going on in the direction of the activity on the road."

"That woman must be as stupid as her grandfather." Mr. Russell hissed back at Mark.

"Charles Logan and his driver kidnapped Ruth MacMillan; and her dog that was with her was killed in the process. That's why all the activity is going on at the Sheriff's office.

"Shannon's grandfather has been wreaking havoc around this town for years." Mr. Russell angrily continued. "He has tried to kidnap Mrs. MacMillan's sons. All the while he is also searching for some mysterious papers his son was supposed to have left behind.

"If the people here find out she's Charles' granddaughter they are not going to give you and Shannon a chance here. You'd better prepare to lose this job. Also, they are positive Shannon's father just up and left."

"What about the activities around welcoming the slaves who escape to Canada?" Mark asked.

"It isn't an illegal activity. They can help the slaves all they want. The Sheriff told me Shannon's grandfather has been sending people down here to cause trouble for several years. He isn't looking for Shannon's father. He is looking for some papers Martin was supposed to bring to his father."

"Oh." Mark said thoughtfully. "They make it sound like the people here are helping to steal property from the Americans." Mark said.

"Listen son, you are one of my favorite nephews. I don't really care whether or not the Negroes come over here, but it isn't illegal. There is nothing we can do about it. People are not considered property in this country.

"That Sheriff's office is full of Indians and Negros but we can't do anything about it. The people down here are accepting these people. If you want to live different, then pack up your wife and go back home."

Mr. Russell packed his briefcase and prepared to leave for his room at the Public House. "I wanted to come down here and see how you were doing and report to your mother, but I will never represent Mr. Logan again. Heed me son, he's causing trouble, stay away from him."

"What happened here?" Shannon asked the deputy who was looking for clues at the side of the road.

"A lady was kidnapped, but we found her, I'm just looking for evidence for the trial." He answered. "You'd better move along now, I'm busy."

"Who was kidnapped?" She asked.

"Listen little lady, I'm busy, you have to move on to wherever you're going."

The deputy was a good friend of Scott's, and after everyone found out about the last Postmaster, most people were hesitant to trust strangers, especially new people in that office.

She continued walking further down the road in the direction where the carriage would have taken Ruth. She had noticed several Indians rode off out of Town and then shortly after, a coloured man overtook her also heading out of Town then turned in to a farm path ahead of her.

"Something's going on." She thought to herself. She followed them down the road and finely reached the sign reading: 'MacMillan Farm'.

"That's her new name." Shannon turned down the lane towards the home of Ruth and her family. Shortly she could see the corner of the bunkhouse and a little further down the lane, the house.

There was a scurry of activity in the yard, and she wasn't noticed right away. A young white boy was working with an Indian man in the corral which kept some cows and horses; she wondered if he was the youngest of her brothers. She could see a chicken coup further along the outside wall of a long log building, which could be a bunkhouse.

"What are you doing here?" A deep voice demanded from behind her.

Stunned, she jumped as she turned around and had to look up to see the face of a large Indian man standing tall with his hands resting on his hips.

"I'm trying to meet my new neighbours." Shannon said nervously.

"Well, follow me." Taima had just returned from the Berry farm to check on things here. He saw Shannon wandering around the yard, and recognized her from the Post Office.

"Scott! Come over here, you have some company."

Several people turned to see who was here.

"What are you doing here, uninvited?" Scott said as he walked towards her. "I told you I would have to work out a visiting time with my wife."

Scott was angry, but tried to remember Shannon was not the person who attacked his family.

"I was walking by, and saw the activity and wanted to see if I could help." Shannon tried to look innocent, but her nervousness betrayed her.

Several people who saw the initial exchange surrounded them to hear.

"After your grandfather kidnapped my wife this morning and his driver killed our dog, I don't want you here, and I don't think my wife or our sons do either." Scott returned. "As a matter of fact, if you need help leaving, I'll see you are escorted home from our property."

Shannon held her breath as her anger swelled; then she blurted out:

"They aren't your sons; they are my father's sons, and my brothers. I have a right to meet them." Shannon shouted.

"But we don't want to know you." A voice calmly spoke from behind her.

She spun around and looked up to face Daniel. "*You are lying!*" Daniel calmly went on. "You said you were just walking and wanted to help; now you are arguing and saying you want to meet your brothers! *Your* grandfather, not mine has been attacking us, and threatening us for years now. No one was polite; no one showed my brother or me they cared about us."

Daniel's voice remained calm, not angry; his face mirrored the sorrow in his heart.

Daniel continued: "They broke into our house to search it; grabbed my friend's little sister on our way home from school. They tied up my brother and mother, and today *your grandfather* came down here in person to kidnap my mother. Not only that, he killed our dog. Now--- here you are--- sneaking around my home." Daniel took a deep breath then continued:

"*Scott MacMillan* is my father, and *Papa Angus MacMillan* is my grandfather. You and your grandfather are *nothing* to us, because you want something we don't have. And furthermore," He looked around at the gathering audience they had attracted. "I don't want anyone else to ask me about Martin Logan. I heard him leave and I heard him say he couldn't stand it here and he was never coming back." Looking back at Shannon and getting eye contact with her he continued: "At this point, as far as I'm concerned he can stay wherever he is."

Silence reigned after Daniel spoke for the first time in front of adults about what had been going on for years. Josh looked down to regard the ground around his feet in sympathy for his friend as he remembered some of their conversations about this subject. He was the only one who had heard any of this over the years.

Scott's eyes watered up when he heard Daniel speak about him and his father. Angus, whose hand rested on Sammy's shoulder had come over and heard the last part of it.

"Young lady." Angus spoke gently. "I think it's time for you to leave this place, you are not welcome here."

"I just wanted to meet my brothers."

"Your brothers have had enough of you and your family, we are not interested." Daniel returned. "*Please leave.*"

He turned his back on her, and then took Sammy's free shoulder and Angus, Daniel and Sammy headed towards Shadow's grave to keep Chance company.

Gordon, who was also watching this exchange, offered to walk her off the property.

Shannon shook off his offer of an arm. "Leave me alone, I can walk home from here." She said as she stomped off down the path towards the main road.

When she was out of earshot, Scott said: "We need someone to follow her, she's on foot and she might duck into the woods and keep searching for something to report."

"I agree," Gordon said. "I'm going home the back way, when I get there I will send Jacob into town to get more help then I will gather my brother and we will help keep watch in the woods."

"I can follow her from the woods;" Taima volunteered. "She'll never know I am there. I'll return when I see her return to the Post Office."

✦

The Sheriff's Office was empty and quiet when Mr. Herbert Russell returned. He had taken some time to gather his thoughts and options. He was worried about how his nephew could become further involved in the wrong side of this ugly situation. He quietly asked Sheriff Pollard if he could see Charles Logan privately to confer.

"May I please meet with you after I see Mr. Logan?" Mr. Russell asked.

"I'll be here when you are ready," The Sheriff replied.

He was then led to the cell where Mr. Logan was being held alone and given a chair to sit on the outside of the bars.

"Where is Mr. Logan's driver, David Tillen, I thought I was representing him too?"

"Mr. Tillen asked to be separated from Mr. Logan; I no longer have them in the same area." The Sheriff answered.

Mr. Russell sat on the chair provided outside the cell while Mr. Logan sat quietly on the cot in the cell wearing the frown which had been his face since he arrived. "It took you long enough to get here." Charles Logan fumed.

After the Sheriff left the room Mr. Russell sat back in his chair and answered: "You're lucky I came here at all. After I heard what you did today I almost left Sandwich Town right away. I thought you were just going to try to see your grandsons?"

Herbert held up his hand and shook his head from side to side as Charles opened his mouth to retort.

"How did that become kidnapping? I told you if she refused, we could work something out. I also thought I would be representing your driver, why has he asked to be removed from you?"

"Are you 'chickening out' too?" Charles answered him. "I said it would be hard to get to see my grandsons and find out what happened to my son. That stupid driver wasn't up to the job. He got afraid when we were arrested."

"What is in those papers you are looking for? The Sheriff says you are more interested in the papers than Martin."

Charles fidgeted in his position on the small cot. "If I can find the papers, maybe they will give a clue as to what happened to Martin." He said.

Charles seemed to find something more interesting to look at than his lawyer. His eyes fixated on a spot outside of the small barred window.

Pausing in reflection, Charles continued. "Martin was supposed to keep a diary of his activities."

"I thought he was running the farm, what other activities could he be doing that would lead to trouble?"

"Nothing, he said he didn't trust the people here, not even that woman." He stood up and started pacing the cell. "Are you going to get me out of here or not?"

"I can't get you out of here today; the judge doesn't come down here until next week. I'm going back to London to notify your personal lawyer. I don't know your history in this area, and he will be able to do a better job for you. The Sheriff said you and your people are known here, and my arguments would be at a disadvantage if I tried to step in now."

"Sniveling idiot." Charles said under his breath.

Herbert Russell heard the comment, but chose not to respond as he stood up picking his chair and left for the outer office. When he shut the door behind him he said: "Can we meet now Sheriff?"

"It's just about supper time," The Sheriff answered, "I was planning to eat at a quiet little shop down the street. Would you like to join me?"

The two men left together for supper.

Shannon slammed the door of the Post Office after her. "I saw my brothers and they have been turned against me! The older one, Daniel, asked me to leave, and that woman's new husband is mean! That terrible woman has made them hate my father and my whole family."

Mark was silent, he had been thinking about the information his uncle told him earlier, and wondered if Shannon knew the things her grandfather had been doing all these years. He was also wondering just what kind of family he had married into.

Shannon's grandfather was proud of arranging this job for him; Mark was thankful for the opportunity and really liked the work. He was also wondering why the people in this town decided not to like them before even meeting them.

Shannon really was pushing the blacksmith and his son with her questions and trying to arrange a meeting this morning. Why didn't she just come out and say she was Martin Logan's daughter? He would like to know what happened in this office before they came.

"Are you listening to me?" Shannon demanded.

Mark looked at her, she was still very angry. He calmly asked if the MacMillan family told her what happened to Ruth and the dog today as the result of her grandfather's visit.

"Oh, my brother had a list of stuff he said my grandfather did, I wasn't listening. My brother said he didn't care if our father came back!" Shannon steamed.

"My uncle came here from the Sheriff's Office and said your grandfather kidnapped his mother this morning and their dog was killed in the process. Did you see Ruth at all today? Did you think to ask the family how they were? Your brothers are probably worried about their mother and grieving over their dog."

"All I saw was their yard was full of Negroes and Indians and some local farmers."

"Maybe you would have had a better reception if you were listening instead of looking. Their neighbours were probably helping with the work, and helping your brothers in their grief." Shannon turned her head away from Mark as he continued: "Are you listening to me? Do you care about your brothers? If you don't — why should they want you around?"

"I'm going to start our evening meal." Shannon huffed out of the office, and left for the living area in the back of the building. Mark thought to himself it was a good thing there were no customers in the office to see her fit of temper.

✦

During the evening meal Uncle Samuel complained that the Sheriff denied him the right to visit Charles Logan.

"I really wanted to give him a piece of my mind!" Uncle Samuel complained.

"You probably would have been arrested for assault!" Ruth laughed. "Then where would you be when the new baby comes!"

"What!" Aunt Elizabeth exclaimed.

Soon all were in a better mood, and Uncle Samuel had to admit the Sheriff was probably right to keep him away from Martin's father.

Ruth's aunt and uncle were both excited to hear the good news. Ruth warned them it was still early and there was a chance the baby might not make it. But everyone clung to the promise of new life. After the meal, they left for home.

Soon the helpers for the activities of the evening started to arrive. Ruth did not speak about the new revelations she, Scott and Sarah and Peter were told today.

✦

Later that evening, the woods surrounding the Berry farm and the MacMillan farm was stirring with activity. Ruth moved to her bed for the evening, she was told by her friends and family to stay there tonight. She had never sat out from helping in all the years they had been welcoming new refugees to Canada.

Amitola told her: "I know you agree the baby is more important, and you have plenty of help. You know, my brother told me he thought you were with child. He seems to know before anyone in our Band when a woman is having a baby, I don't know how he does it." She smiled.

Outside, Daniel and some of the local men prepared for tonight's visitors. Jacob Burke was helping to prepare for the refugees for the first time tonight. Daniel and Jacob finished the bunkhouse while the older men patrolled the grounds for a safe evening.

Jacob was feeling proud; his father and the other men had enough confidence in him to be a responsible worker tonight.

Scott was with Peter at the cove and would be one of the people who accompanied the refugees from the cove to the bunkhouse. There was no peace in the woods tonight, they hadn't needed this many people for an arrival since the time Ruth and Sammy were captured and held hostage in the house.

When the three men and two women arrived at the cove that evening a scurry of activity was set into place. The refugees were quickly offloaded from the rowboat and the conductor headed back to Detroit with some fish Josh, Jacob and Daniel had caught earlier.

The story was, the conductor was fishing and just returned. As time passed, the people who were helping from Detroit were taking a bigger risk. People crossing the river were being watched carefully, and the conductors from Detroit and the other Americans were risking their lives and freedom to help the refugees enter Canada.

Tonight, the new refugees had a good crossing. They were startled to see so many people patrolling the woods and the two farms, but they said they felt safe. The two women stayed in the bunkhouse at the Berry farm and the men were moved to the MacMillan farm and the bunkhouse there.

All the new people were provided with a hot meal and all they needed to start their life in Canada. This time, two of the men chose to stay in Sandwich Town, but the others wanted to continue further inland.

At dawn the next morning, the women were moved to the MacMillan farm and joined the third man, who was married to one of the women. The new Canadians were loaded into the wagon and accompanied by two men from the Band and left for the Chatham area.

Later in the morning, Peter arrived at the farm with his buckboard and took the two men who chose to stay in Sandwich, Adam and John, to meet Rev Hubbs and his family. They would help the men start their new life here.

✦

At 9:00 a.m. Mark Miller opened the Post Office. Shortly after his uncle, Herbert Russell entered the office.

"Did you talk to Shannon last evening?" Herbert asked.

"I told her what you said yesterday; she went to the MacMillan farm and was chased off by her brother Daniel, and Ruth's new husband Scott. They figured out she was Martin Logan's daughter and don't want her around at all. I don't understand her; she started an argument with them.

"They told her what her grandfather had done, but she didn't ask how Ruth was, or that she was sorry their dog was killed, or even how the boys were doing. She doesn't seem to care about them. I don't know why she even wants to see them. Shannon's attitude confuses me."

"Last evening," Herbert interjected. "I went to dinner with the Sheriff to try to figure out what is going on in this place. The Sheriff doesn't understand why Charles Logan is still looking for his son here. The whole community doesn't know anything about those papers he is looking for, and why he is being so aggressive towards Ruth and her sons.

"He says the people here are definitely helping refugees who come from the United States, but since that is not illegal; he has no problem with it. He says he has had to arrest and accompany 'catchers' from the United States and accompany them back to Detroit by ferry. Some of them have even attacked people here who were helping,"

"Is Ruth and her family a part of this?" Mark asked.

"I didn't even ask that question Mark, and don't you either. No one here is going to offer to give you information that could put themselves or anyone else in danger, especially the way Shannon's grandfather is acting. I think her grandfather is trying to stop the things going on here, and information about the activities here is what your wife's father had in those papers.

I think Mr. Logan is a dangerous man, and you should get yourself and your wife away from here and him." Herbert sighed, and then continued. "I'm leaving now, I will contact Charles' lawyer when I get home, and I will not be back unless you need me.

I will not involve myself in Charles' side of this mess, and I advise you to stay out of it too. What Charles is up to is not moral, or legal. Say my goodbyes to Shannon."

Mark walked his Uncle Herbert out of the Post Office, and watched him mount his horse and ride down the dirt road towards Amherstburg, then London.

Shannon met him when he returned to the office.

"Where did your uncle go? She asked.

"He went back to London, he will arrange for your grandfather's old lawyer to represent him in this case. Uncle Herbert thinks he is at a disadvantage because he doesn't have the complete history of the quarrel." Mark responded flatly.

"Huhh. My grandfather thought he was some big shot lawyer who could get things done!" Shannon huffed.

"Your grandfather didn't take his advice, participated in illegal activities, and my uncle thinks he is not being truthful to him. My uncle won't work like that. I'm going to tender my resignation here, we won't be accepted in this town with the mistrust the people here feel for us." Mark responded quietly.

"I'm not leaving! I'm not giving up! I'm going to find out what is going on here, and what happened to my father. That brat brother of mine said he doesn't care, well, I do!"

Mark chose to remain silent in response her remark. Just then a customer entered and the conversation was stopped in its tracks.

The boys got up from the table and headed outdoors to start their chores for the day. Peter had just left to bring the two new men to Rev Hubbs and Scott and Ruth were alone at the table. Amitola and her friend were in the bunkhouse gathering linens to wash and prepare to do the chores Ruth would usually do on the morning after a landing.

"You haven't said anything about what I told you yesterday about Martin's death." Scott opened.

"I don't know what to think. I fully understand why the men wanted to keep his death quiet. I've been angry at Martin for years for not even contacting me or my sons. I have to let go of that anger. The contents of the books and the maps, however, I shudder to think what Martin, his father and his friends would have done with that information." Ruth had been thinking all night about the information Scott told her yesterday.

"When I was telling you what was found yesterday I thought you looked angry and was wondering where your anger was focused."

"At first, I was angry because my Uncle Samuel didn't include me with the few who knew. After I thought about it, I realized I would have told my captors at the house here, when Sammy and I were tied up in the kitchen. Those two men were waving guns at and around us, yelling at me and calling me a liar. I also knew, I would have told Mr. Logan yesterday when he had the gun aimed at my face.

"Even now, I wonder if I should have been told. I know keeping the secret is the only way to stop the Chippewa people and the Negroes from being blamed for Martin's death. My prayer is that I can be trusted with the knowledge. I don't even want to think about what would have happened if Martin had been able to deliver those books and maps. I'm glad they were destroyed."

March 1849
CHAPTER 7

THE WAGON WITH THE SPECIAL SECRET HIDING PLACE LUMbered down the clear well-worn road between Chatham and Amherstburg. The four men in the secret compartment were told they were not safe in Chatham and should move on to Toronto where they would be able to find good jobs and be safe. The space in the compartment was tight with the three men, and their coats, at least body heat helped to shield them against the cold air outside. The two men driving the wagon hunched forward against the wind.

They noticed a group of four Chippewa men covered with extra blankets against the weather riding on horseback towards them. Apenimon's son, Chogan (Blackbird) and his friends, Dyami (Eagle), Kohana (Swift), and Nodin (Wind) were travelling to a meeting on Walpole Island in Lake St. Clair near the mouth of the St. Clair River.

"The Indians around here help moving the slaves; I hope these ones aren't nosey." John Daily said to his partner. "We should be in Amherstburg by this afternoon."

"Hello friend." Nodin called, a cloud of breath surrounded his head and trailed behind him as the two parties passed on the road.

The two men driving the wagon just nodded, each with a scowl and puffs from their breath rising above their faces in the cold morning air.

After they passed, Chogan said: "The wagon looks like the ones built by Peter and Gordon. Do any of you know the drivers?"

The four young men stopped their horses and looked at each other. The horses snorted steam and clumped their hooves. The men turned back and then regarded the wagon heading in the direction of Amherstburg. Kohana commented on how it seemed to be 'riding heavy'.

It should be empty heading back home. Lately, some of the refugees have mysteriously disappeared. Could this wagon hold the answer to the question? The young men decided this problem couldn't be ignored and they should change their plans: they all headed towards the woods. Chogan and Dyami took the short cut towards Amherstburg to tell Samuel Patterson, and Kohana and Nodin headed towards Sandwich Town to tell Peter.

✦

The two men rode into Sandwich Town after three years of being away. They were dressed for the late winter weather with overcoats, scarves and hats. They secured rooms at the Public house, and then made a short visit to the Post Office. Their next stop was to the blacksmith shop where a young man stood over the anvil hammering a horseshoe into the correct form. The men enjoyed the heat coming from the open fire which stood beside his work station as he expertly moved the shoe in and out of the fire to adjust the shape.

Daniel, now eighteen years old, stopped his work and looked up to ask the two men: "Hello, can I help you?"

"Yes, may we speak to Mr. MacMillan Sr. or Jr.?" The older man asked.

Daniel turned to the back of the shop and called: "Poppa there's some men here to see you."

Shortly, Scott came out to see who was there. "Oh, I didn't expect to see you back here."

"May we talk in private?" Herbert Russell asked.

"Sure, come in the back to our office." Scott answered.

Once in the office, Mark Miller introduced his Uncle Herbert Russell to Scott. The men removed their outer clothes and hung them on hooks hanging on the wall by the door, and then took the chairs which were offered to them.

Mark then went on to say. "Mr. MacMillan, I was wondering how you and your family are doing. I know I apologised to you for my part in the events from three years ago, but I also want to say, since then I have matured as a man."

Not giving Scott a chance to respond, he went on: "When I handed in my resignation to the Post Office for the job here, I begged to be given another chance in another town. I was given a job in Chatham, and since being there, I have had the chance to know many of the refugees, who have made the trip to Canada through this area and have heard their stories. I now understand what is going on here, and I am embarrassed by my own actions and prejudices, and Shannon and her family's actions.

He looked down, then directly in Scott's eyes. "Shannon did not make the trip to Toronto with me to hand in my resignation. She stopped in London and moved back into her mother's home. We have been living separate lives since then. I heard she and her brother went out West to see if they can find out anything about their father."

By this time, Angus had joined Scott and the visitors and heard the last statement. He interjected at this point: "It's been almost thirteen years since Martin left son, I'm thinking the trail might be very cold."

"I've told them that also. They should have been looking elsewhere years ago rather than concentrate their efforts here." Herbert added. "I'm so proud of my nephew in that he's been following my advice and staying away from Shannon and her family."

"We believe the Logan family were not so interested in finding Martin as they were in finding the 'papers' he was supposed to have delivered. My prayer is that Shannon, her mother and her siblings find peace." Angus added.

"I wanted to tell you both about my personal growth, but I also wanted to see how you and your family have been faring these last three years." Mark asked. "How is your wife and how are the children doing with the loss of their dog?"

"It has been a peaceful time." Scott answered. "There have been no incidents stemming from the Logan family in London. My wife was not doing well after the attack, but that was because she was with child, and she had to stay quiet for the rest of her term.

"I moved my family in Town, my father and I have fixed up a house we had at the back of the shop. The farm where we were living has been sold to a local farmer. I feel my family is safer, here in Town. We had a son, and named him after my father, Angus." Scott smiled as he looked at his father and thought of the joy little Angus has brought to their lives.

Scott continued: "The children were devastated at the loss of their dog, Shadow, especially since he was just left in the road to die. We were glad one of our sons' friends found him and brought him home, at least we were able to take care of him until he died." Scott said.

"It was a bad day for sure." Angus added. "The next door neighbour's dog was Shadow's brother and he was devastated also, we were afraid he would die of a broken heart. God was willing and we were able to find two new puppies, one for the next door neighbours to give their dog someone to care for, and one for Daniel and Sammy and now, little Angus to love."

"I'm glad your family is doing well." Mark said. "I have been corresponding with Abraham Hubbs, the new Postmaster here. My uncle and I will be meeting with him and his family for dinner tonight. Our correspondence has helped me understand how things are down here."

"I also had much to learn about the refugee situation and about the Native People." Herbert said. "I was against how Charles Logan was acting, but was also afraid to trust people who didn't look like me.

"Now I know we are all God's children and He loves all of His children. I would like to add my apology to my nephew's for my attitude when I came down here. As well, I would like to apologise for initially agreeing to be Charles Logan's attorney.

"We don't expect your family to trust us after how we met, especially since all the anger was pointed at you and your family. We beg you to consider forgiving our involvement at some point." Herbert Russell was sincere in his apology.

"If your wife and sons will see us, we would like to apologise to them also." Mark said.

"Thank you for this visit." Scott answered. "If you're still in Town, come back tomorrow for the noon meal, I'll talk to my family tonight at our evening meal."

✦

Peter met Kohana and Nodin as they rode down the path from the main road in front of his farm.

"We passed a heavy wagon heading towards Amherstburg on the road from Chatham. It looks like one of yours. We are thinking that's the way the refugees are becoming missing." Nodin reported breathlessly.

"Yes," Kohana added. "We were travelling with Chogan and Dyami; they have left for Mr. Patterson's farm."

"Good." Peter said. "Josh, I need you, saddle our horses, we have to travel to Amherstburg. Adam, call your mother and Anna out here please."

The now seven year old Adam ran into the house to call his mother and Anna, now thirteen, into the yard. Peter and Josh, eighteen like his best friend Daniel, mounted their horses. Peter quickly told Sarah and

Anna what was happening and then the father and son joined the other two young men and rode away from the farm.

When they passed the Band property, Kohana called: "I'm telling my people, we can add some more people to help."

"Good idea." Peter called.

As they passed the Patterson farm, Samuel and some of his men were exiting his property with Chogan and Dyami.

"I figure they will head for the port to catch one of the large boats going to Ohio." Samuel told Peter.

"That's my thinking too." Peter replied. "Somehow, we will have to watch the port without being seen,"

✦

"Momma, the signal light from Detroit is flashing!" Anna called to her mother.

Sarah rushed to the big window facing the river and lit their signal light. "Anna, please saddle your horse, I need you to go to Uncle Jackson's, next door, and then to Town. I don't think your father and Josh will be back in time to receive refugees tonight."

After the message was received — there would be three new people coming, Sarah told Anna:

"Be sure to take the back way both to Uncle Jackson's and to Town, and be careful in Town. Be sure not to talk in front of strangers to Uncle Scott; ask to see him in private before you tell him anything about tonight's travellers."

"Okay Momma, I'll be careful." Anna was proud. This is the first time she was able to travel to Town by herself, and on such an important mission.

✦

When Anna entered the Blacksmith's shop Daniel called to her: "Anna, how are things going? Who is with you, is Josh coming soon?"

"I have a message for your Poppa." She answered solemnly.

"He and Grandfather are with some men in the office right now. Wait here while I get him."

Noticing the expression on her face, Daniel knew what it was about. He put down his tools and turned for the office, just as Scott, Angus and the two visitors exited.

"I pray gentlemen, your visit here will be positive." Angus said to the two men.

Anna waited until the door shut after the men, and then said: "My Momma has sent me here with a message for tonight."

"Daniel, join Anna and us in the office." Scott told them.

"You go ahead son, I'll stay here and take over this job." Angus volunteered.

Once in the office, Anna said: "This morning Kohana and Nodin came to the farm and said one of our wagons carrying refugees was heading from Chatham to Amherstburg. My Poppa thinks that is how some refugees are becoming missing. My Poppa and Josh joined them; they are going to Amherstburg to see what is happening.

"Just now we got a signal from Detroit saying three people are coming tonight, and my Momma is worried that Poppa and Josh will not be back in time for their arrival. Can you help us?"

"Of course we will Anna." Scott took both Anna's hands in his. "You did a good job reporting to us dear. Daniel, I want you to accompany Anna home now, and see if Auntie Sarah needs any help right now. Make sure you take the back path. Anna, did you take the back path here?"

"Yes, I did Uncle Scott, Momma had me tell Uncle Jackson too before I came here."

"Good, you two be on your way now, I'll get some help together and be at your cove tonight in plenty of time." Scott said, as his mind filled with plans to gather more help.

✦

"That must be them coming now; I recognize the wagon as one of ours." Peter said.

"Let Jeffery and me go down there first." Samuel said. "They will be more on guard with you Peter."

"Yes, you're right." Peter answered.

As Samuel and his foreman, Jeffery travelled down to the dock, the others were signaled by Peter to hold back. The party of rescuers were spread out, two by two to cover the length of the dock. The boat leaving for Ohio had not arrived yet, but was nearing the dock.

When he became close to the wagon, Samuel called to the men driving: "Hail, are you planning to travel on this boat to Ohio?"

Immediately bangs and yelling came from the secret compartment under the bed of the wagon:

"NO! HELP! LET US OUT OF HERE!"

Samuel's foreman signalled the rest of the rescue party to join them. Peter and all the others rushed down to the wagon. Samuel sent Jeffery to bring the Sheriff.

"This is my wagon." Peter said as he arrived on the scene; "someone stole it last month."

"We didn't steal your wagon, we found it." John answered.

Josh and Nodin opened the secret compartment and helped the cramped four men out of the small compartment to freedom again.

"T'ank you, those men tol us we should go to Toronto, it wer safer."

"If you want to go to Toronto we can take you there, but you don't have to hide in the compartment of the wagon." Josh said.

Apenimon and several others from the Band had arrived just in time to see the men leave the compartment of the wagon.

"No, su's," Said one of the other men. "We hab friends in Chatham, these men tol us people was after us from down South. Peter, is that you? You hep'd when we fust arrived here! I'z Joe from bout ten yars ago."

"I remember you! Glad we could help again!" Peter continued. "Apenimon, I recognise those horses as ours. I'm thinking we should just let these two fend for themselves without horses, and take the wagon and our horses back."

"Father," Chogan interjected. "I recognise this one man as John Daily, who works for David Johnson and carried out work for Charles Logan."

"Peter, he also helped kidnap Anna several years ago. These two men kidnapped the people we just rescued, and it should be reported."

"I have already sent Jeffery for the Sheriff." Samuel said. "They should be arriving back here shortly."

Apenimon had his men tie John and his cohort's hands with rope to confine them until the Sheriff from Amherstburg arrived. During which there was a flurry of complaints from John and his partner, and relieved comments from the four men who were confined and threatened to be sent back to the United States.

Shortly the Sheriff and his deputy arrived and arrested the two men for kidnapping and took them away. Samuel and Jeffery accompanied the party as witnesses. The final decision for the four men was that Chogan, Dyami, Kohana and Nodin would take them back to Chatham riding in the bed of the wagon this time. After the meeting in Walpole Island the young men would return the wagon to Gordon's farm to be checked in case it needed repairs. The other rescuers were then free to return home.

Peter and Josh stopped at Samuel's farm to tell Elizabeth everything turned out all right and Samuel would be along later. When they stopped at the Band to see Siwili, Peter and Josh were told about the expected new arrivals tonight.

✦

At the Abraham Hubbs home, preparations were being made for company tonight. Effie, Abraham's wife, was busy preparing the meal in the kitchen of their small, two bedroom apartment at the back of the Post Office.

"At least there is a nice dining room." She thought. "Later this spring the weather will be nice enough to entertain outdoors at the picnic table Peter made for us as a housewarming present. I'm so thankful Abe got this position after Mark and Shannon left."

It was such a nice apartment, and entertaining in the back yard in summertime was relaxing. She loved this place and enjoyed making it a real home for her and Abe. Effie didn't know what to think about this apparent change of heart Mark said he experienced but her husband was willing to give him the benefit of the doubt for now.

The Post Office must be busy today; she could hear the tinkle of the front door bells ring several times already. Effie decided to make a pot of tea and see if Abe wanted to have some, or maybe even take a break. Their daughter, Beverly was still down for her nap and Henry and John were across the street playing with Angus in the back of the Blacksmith Shop. It was a good time to relax before the final preparations for company tonight. It was nice of Ruth to agree to keep the boys this afternoon while she made her preparations.

When she had the tea steeping in the pot she poked her head in the office and asked Abe if he would like some. Scott was with him and they were talking serious.

"Effie, is there enough for Scott? We will take our break in the back with you." Abe said.

When they sat at the dining Room table in the apartment, Abe told Scott: "I really don't know whether those two can be trusted or not. Some say Mark is helping the new people, but then since this past summer, we've been experiencing the disappearances of some people from the Chatham area."

"Okay Abe, maybe you should not help us tonight, just have your dinner and not say anything to them about it. I still have to talk to Ruth about whether or not she will see those men tomorrow. As far as I'm concerned that is entirely up to her."

"I'll sound them out tonight, but this is too important to leave the decision to one visit. Personally, I wouldn't want them anywhere near Berry's Cove, or anyone who might think they could be trusted." Abe said thoughtfully.

"I agree with you Abe, we will miss you tonight. I didn't want to leave you out of the information chain." Scott knew what would result from this meeting, but he knew he had to make the visit. "Have a good time tonight; I know the cooking will be wonderful Effie!" He called as he left.

As Scott walked across the street towards his shop, he went over the plans for tonight in his head. He had contacted the Sheriff and Seamus and his son. Jackson sent word Abe's brother Hank and several others from Sandwich First Baptist as well as some local farmers would be in attendance to help.

He had mentioned Peter and Josh's errand to Abe in the Post Office before Effie came out and asked them to tea. He, Ruth and his father prayed earlier about that errand and their prayer hid in the back of his mind all day. Their prayer asked for the safety of everyone involved and the outcome would be for the rescue of the new Canadians. He would leave after the evening meal to meet Daniel at the Berry farm. Maybe Peter and Josh would be back after all.

Sheriff Lawrence from Amherstburg didn't know what to think of his newest charges. The two men seemed to think it was their duty to return as many of the refugees from slavery as possible to the United States. He received the statements from Samuel and Jeffery and let them go home. He saw the wagon which Peter said he built, and he recognised it as one of the ones used around this area. He talked to the prisoners who were freed by the rescue party.

Still, his two new prisoners said they were in the right. The Sheriff knew the law was clear. It was legal for the refugees to come here from the United States, and it was not legal to kidnap anyone and send them anywhere.

What really made him wonder was, the men were both from London, and what were they doing in Chatham? He remembered the name John Daily from years ago, and was glad Samuel said he would contact his investigator, Bradley Cummings. Mr. Cummings was working with his son, Sullivan now, but the boy was just as good as his father.

In any case, these two could wait until the Judge came to Town after the weekend. Maybe Sullivan would be back from his information-gathering trip to London before the judge arrived.

✦

Peter and Josh saw Kajika before he noticed them as they came slowly down the path and around the house and into the barnyard.

"Kajika will tell us what is planned and what still needs to be done." Peter told his son.

"I hope there's some fishing to be done." Josh smiled as he told his father, "I could use some quiet time under that big old Maple tree!"

"Hi! How did things go in Amherstburg?" Kajika called.

"We were able to stop four people from being sent south. One of the men, we knew from a crossing some years ago." Josh answered him.

"Good! We have three more refugees coming here tonight." Kajika told them.

"We heard at the Band Kajika. What can we do?"

"I think if you don't let your wife feed you your evening meal and rest, you and I will both be in trouble!" Kajika smiled, "Here she comes."

"Thank the Good Lord you are back safely! Both of you get washed up and come in here and eat before you do anything else!" Sarah was relieved to see her two men back safely.

Anna brought some clean towels out to the well for her father and Josh and told them: "Daniel and Jacob are at the cove fishing for the conductor tonight." Josh groaned. "Uncle Scott and some of the Town men will be here later. Uncle Jackson is coordinating for security from the Band, the Church and our neighbours."

"I was hoping to get some fishing in." Josh said.

"Thanks Anna, it sounds like everything is organized for us this time." Peter told her.

Later, after his arrival, Scott told Peter and Josh to sit out this time. "You two have had a full day already. Let us handle the landing tonight without you."

"Thanks Scott, I think I'll take you up on your offer this time." Peter told him. "Can we meet tomorrow morning? Something happened you should know about."

"Here too Peter, I have to tell you something too. I'll be here first thing tomorrow morning."

Peter and Josh were still eating at the kitchen table when the boat came around the mouth of the cove into safe waters within. Anna called from her sitting spot by the big window. "Here they come!"

The two tired men watched the activities from the table as they finished their evening meal. They saw the local helpers welcome the three new people. They scooped them from the rowboat and whisked the new people to the path leading to Jackson's farm and the bunkhouse.

Daniel and Jacob gave the fish to the conductor who took them back as a cover for his trip. Peter was proud of how the welcome effort came together even though he could not be involved this time.

He smiled at Sarah and said: "This is a dream-come-true for me. The whole effort came together without me. Thank you for spreading the word, and thank all these friends who have the same dream as us."

"Poppa, I hope you don't need me tomorrow morning, Daniel, Jacob and I would like to go fishing early tomorrow morning. We can provide fish for all our homes for breakfast tomorrow." There was no way Josh would give up his fishing time, or the chance to swap stories with his friends.

"Son," Sarah added. "Don't forget some extra fish for Uncle Jackson and Auntie Cissy; they will need extra for the new people."

"Right Momma! Do you mind Poppa?" He asked again.

"It's fine with me son, Daniel will probably be coming with Uncle Scott. Sarah, Scott wants to come early in the morning for a meeting with me, apparently something happened in Town today."

"I haven't heard anything. I've been so busy with preparations for tonight and the family I haven't thought or talked about anything else."

"We'll find out tomorrow." Peter said.

"What's the meeting between Uncle Scott and my father this morning?" Josh asked.

"Two men came to Town yesterday and want to meet with my family."

"Who?"

"Do you remember my sister's husband who used to be the Postmaster when my Momma was kidnapped?"

"I remember," Josh solemnly looked down as he remembered that day. "What a horrible day. What do they want?" Josh answered.

"They want to meet my Momma and us; they are asking to be forgiven for their part in the day. They asked Poppa Scott if they could come by for the afternoon meal today. They have been corresponding with Abe and had the evening meal last night with them."

"Oh," Josh looked over to Daniel. "I wondered where Abe was working last night; usually he helps near the cove."

"That's all my story, tell me about yesterday and the rescue; yesterday was such a busy day." Daniel said.

Jacob was needed at home this morning, and Josh and Daniel were alone to exchange stories about the rescue and the visit. A similar conversation was happening in the Berry kitchen.

"Can we trust those two men? Did they really have a change-of-heart?" Sarah asked.

"That's the big question." Scott said. "It really makes me think even more now, since Peter told me John Daily was a part of the team who took those men from Chatham yesterday."

"I think you should meet with those men this morning and tell them what happened in Amherstburg yesterday. See how they react to the news John was involved." Sarah said.

"Actually," Peter added slowly. "I think our two families should meet with them together. If Ruth feels threatened, all of us together will give her reassurance, and then Mark and his uncle will know we are a united front."

"I agree; that's a wonderful idea." Scott said. "After all, your family and security has been affected just as much as ours." Scott stood up.

"This meeting is over. I will tell Ruth about our decision right now." He smiled as he added: "Please tell Daniel, he will be expected home for the afternoon meal."

"Our whole family will be there too." Sarah said.

After hearing the Berry's would attend, Ruth felt better about agreeing to the afternoon meal meeting. Sarah, Anna and Adam arrived early to help with the cooking and preparations for the extra family. Peter and Josh arrived just before the visitors were about to arrive. Angus, Scott and Daniel closed the shop for the meeting when Mark and Herbert arrived. Sammy was working at Jackson's farm and promised to come home for the meeting.

"Kajika and Chogan are at our farm to keep an eye on things." Sarah volunteered.

"Good, even if we think these men are sincere, it will take time for me to trust them. I really do hope they are sincere. God will let us know how we should respond to them." Ruth answered.

"Maybe we should pray now, before things get started. Anna, Adam, Angus, come here please we all need to pray now."

"Thank you Sarah now is good."

While the prayer was being said inside, introductions were being made in the Blacksmith Shop. Scott introduced the two visitors to Peter and Josh, and the official introduction was made for Daniel whom they saw working yesterday.

149

Mark immediately apologised to Daniel for the behaviour of his wife on the day she visited the farm. Daniel hung his head and remained silent. It was a bad day for all of them, and Shannon's visit didn't help matters at all.

Daniel said: "My Poppa told us you came to apologise before you left Town. He also said you were concerned about my Momma and all of us because Shadow was killed. Thank you for that." Finally he said: "My Poppa also said you have had a change of heart towards what we do here."

"Let's go to our home behind the shop." Angus said as he gathered Daniel and Josh, an arm on each young man's shoulder and led the way.

Sammy had joined the family in the house by the time the other men arrived for the meeting. Introductions were made all around again.

Ruth had everyone sit around the large table made by Scott and Peter. The Berry and MacMillan families had been visiting back and forth sharing holidays for several years now. Today Ruth and Sarah had assigned seating for everyone.

At first, nothing of consequence was said. Awkward requests for the passing of food and superficial pleasantries were the extent of the conversation. Even little Angus picked up on the uneasy atmosphere.

Finally, Herbert said: "My nephew and I did not come down here to try to insert ourselves into your life, or to spy. We want you to know we are sorry for the part we played three years ago when Ruth was kidnapped, and your dog was killed. I intend to go back to my legal practice in London, and Mark intends to go back to his job as Postmaster in Chatham. We just hope you can eventually forgive us for our part in the events of that day."

"Thank you for your comments Herbert, but maybe you and Mark are not aware of things that have been happening in Chatham, and one large event that happened yesterday." The Grandfather Angus said. "Peter do you want to tell these men what happened yesterday?"

Peter sat erect in his chair and spoke. "Since the beginning of last summer we have been hearing that several refugees have been disappearing from the Chatham area."

"Yes, I have been hearing that too, from some of my new friends in the area." Mark said.

Peter continued: "Yesterday, we got word that one of our wagons, which was stolen two weeks ago, was loaded with people and heading for Amherstburg to meet a boat going to Ohio. My son, Josh and I joined a rescue party and were able to assist in saving four men from being sent back to the United States and slavery.

"One of the men who abducted these men was John Daily, Shannon's uncle. John was actively involved with Charles Logan's several assaults here. We are wondering if you knew about any of this."

Mark lowered his head, then looked Peter straight in the eyes and quietly said:

"No, I didn't know. I can understand how you would think as much." He took a deep breath and continued. "I heard Charles Logan died in prison last year. Anna-Lynn, John's sister and Shannon's mother is a vengeful person. In the past, she has been a force behind many of Charles' actions.

"I think she is also behind Shannon's and her brothers' decision to go west and look for their father. I wouldn't be surprised if she is also helping John with his plans.

"She and Shannon were both vicious towards me when I left the marriage, and refused to continue helping them. I'm sorry I married into that family, and I only wish I could find a way to divorce Shannon."

"I believe you Mark." Ruth said. "I know how it feels to love someone and then find out you didn't know them at all. Five years after Martin left my Uncle sent investigators to London. That's when I found out I wasn't even married. Martin was already married to Anna-Lynn, and Shannon was born when Martin and I were married here. I found out that day he only married me to try to get control of my Uncle's property and money. At least, I have two wonderful sons from him."

The rest of the evening went smoother, since the hard conversation was done. Young Angus and the other children seemed to sense the ease in tension and started acting more natural.

Mark and Herbert had a chance to play with the new MacMillan dog, Dusty before they left for the evening. It turned out to be a productive evening after all.

September 1851
EPILOGUE

Ruth sat at the table outdoors in the yard where she spent so many years. Her chair faced the familiar barn and bunkhouse. The comfortable outdoors wooden lawn chair was made by Jackson and Sammy.

Sammy was spending several hours a week now, after school working and learning alongside Jackson. They had made four chairs to augment the benches which had originally surrounded the table when Ruth and her family lived here. Cissy and Willis Jackson had really made this farm their own.

When Cissy gave her the grand tour on her first visit back shortly after Angus was born, Ruth knew. It was their home now. Cissy made all new curtains and Jackson and Gordon built beds for their children, Leroy and the new baby Willis, named after his daddy, and several pieces of furniture for the rooms. After that visit she and Scott discussed the matter. As a result, she told Uncle Samuel she and Scott decided not to move back here. Within a year, Uncle Samuel had his lawyers sign the land over to Jackson, the same as he had done for Peter. Uncle Samuel said it this way; the land near Berry's Cove should stay in the hands of people friendly to the cause.

She is happy in the house Scott and his father built behind the Blacksmith Shop. There is plenty of room for them and their three sons. After Martin's daughter, Shannon visited the farm the afternoon of her abduction Daniel and Sammy wanted nothing to do with any of the Logan family. Scott, at the request of Daniel and Sammy legally adopted the two boys, and they had been using the MacMillan last name ever since.

Sullivan Cummings, the son of Uncle Samuel's investigator, Bradley, was instrumental in identifying the ring of people who were behind the several abductions in the Chatham area. John Daly and his partner are still in jail for participating in the crime the local people were involved in stopping.

As far as Martin's two oldest children, Shannon and Gabriel, they have not been heard of since they went west to find their father at their mother's request. Anna Lynn, Martin's wife and John Daly's sister, developed heart problems and is confined to her bed. Her youngest daughter, Jeanne and her family have been taking care of her for over a year now.

Mark Miller, Shannon's estranged husband has been keeping in touch with Jeanne and keeping Scott and her up to date with information. He still seems to be sincere.

Ruth's pensive mood brightened when Cissy brought soup and rolls to the table for them and called Leroy and the two little ones for the afternoon meal. Angus and Willis ran from their game in the yard to the table. The two little ones had become great friends and Cissy and she visited each other to promote the friendship, just as Sarah and she had done for Daniel and Josh.

While they were eating, they noticed Jacob Burke riding down the lane on his horse.

"Hi Auntie Ruth, Auntie Cissy, I have the new edition of the "Voice of the Fugitive" hot off the presses!"

"Wonderful Jacob, have you delivered ours to the Shop yet?"

"No Auntie Ruth, Mr. Bibb was going there himself today. I have to be off to the next subscriber now; have a good day." Jacob called and waved as he left them.

"Sometimes when I read this here paper, I see notices concerning people I knew when I was a child in the South. I'm hoping to hear something about my sister. Before my Momma and I were able to leave, she was sold to a plantation further south. I was only a child when Momma and I came here."

"I remember you telling me she was sold. I hope you hear something one day. That new Fugitive Slave Law the American government passed last year has made things harder for people to bear." Ruth said.

"Yes, now our friends in the Northern States who have been helping us are legally responsible to officially assist marshals in recapturing their slaves."

"I often wonder when this will end. Scott and Peter talk about freedom for all in the United States in our lifetime, I pray it will happen."

Cissy looked around her and mused: "Willis says this is evidence the South knows the end is near. He says in a battle; the biggest 'push' happens when the aggressor knows he is beaten."

Ruth sighed, "As long as it takes, we will continue our work here."

"As long as it takes." Cissy answered.

Post Script

THE AMERICAN CIVIL WAR STARTED IN **1861** AND ENDED IN 1865. Emancipation in the United States was official for all states when the 13th Amendment was passed on January 31, 1865. It was ratified by all the states by December 6, 1865. At that time many of the refugees living in Canada chose to return to their homes in the hopes of finding their relatives, or just starting over. Many chose to stay here in Canada. I believe our country is richer for it!

Sandwich First Baptist Church: is still an active church and standing on Peter Street, just east of Prince Road in Old Sandwich Town, West Windsor. The building was completed in 1851. It is a designated historical site now and is a stop on many bus tours of the area.

Sandwich Methodist Church: is now known as Bedford United Church. It is still an active church and the present brick building was constructed in 1906 and also has a heritage designation. When the United Church of Canada was founded in 1925, it was a merger of the Methodist Church, the Congregational Church and the Presbyterian Church. It is located on Sandwich Street west of Brock.

St. John's Anglican Church and Churchyard: is still an active church and is located on the corner of Sandwich and Brock. The church yard is one of the oldest cemeteries in the community and is located west of the building. The original building was burned in the war of 1812 and its replacement was built in 1819, which would have been used during the time of this story. The present building was constructed in 1871. This building also has a heritage designation.

Our Lady of the Assumption Roman Catholic Church: is located on the corner of Huron Church Road and University (a continuation of Sandwich Street) and faces the Detroit River. The church is the oldest continuous parish in Ontario and dates back to 1728. It is still an active church today. The current church was completed in 1842 during the time this story occurred; it also has a heritage designation. This church is east of most of the action in this story.

The Local Chippewa Band: I have never been able to find a positive location of the Band at that time. I believe it was in the area west of Sandwich Town around the present LaSalle and taking in the present Ojibway Park area. At the present time the local native peoples live in the local communities.

The Old Black Cemetery: I have heard there was one in an area between Amherstburg and La Salle but to my knowledge none has been found yet.

The Voice of the Fugitive: The first black-owned and operated newspaper in Canada. Founded by Henry Bibb who was a refugee from slavery. This was an abolitionist newspaper founded in 1851.